Tyrant of the Tides

Tyrant of the Tides
From Italian *Topolino* #3000, 2013
Writer: Francesco Artibani
Artist: Corrado Mastantuono
Colorists: Mirka Andolfo with Erik Rosengarten
Letterers: Nicole and Travis Seitler
Translation and Dialogue: Thad Komorowski

Astray For a Day
From Finnish *Aku Ankka* #23/2012
Writer, Artist, and Letterer: William Van Horn
Colorist: Digikore Studios

The Substitute Santa of Strathbungo
From Norwegian *Donald Julealbum* #4, 2013
Writers: Knut Nærum and Tormod Løkling
Artist: Arild Midthun
Colorist: Digikore Studios
Letterer: Jesse Post
Dialogue: Byron Erickson

Scientific Sculptor
From *Donald Duck* Sunday comic Strip, 1963
Writer: Bob Karp
Artist and Letterer: Al Taliaferro
Colorist: Digikore Studios

Special thanks to Eugene Paraszczuk, Julie Dorris, Carlotta Quattrocolo, Manny Mederos, Chris Troise, Roberto Santillo, Camilla Vedove, and Stefano Ambrosio.

ISBN: 978-1-63140-887-8   20 19 18 17   1 2 3 4

www.IDWPUBLISHING.com

Ted Adams, CEO & Publisher • Greg Goldstein, President & COO • Robbie Robbins, EVP/Sr. Graphic Artist • Chris Ryall, Chief Creative Officer • David Hedgecock, Editor-in-Chief • Laurie Windrow, Senior Vice President of Sales & Marketing • Matthew Ruzicka, CPA, Chief Financial Officer • Lorelei Bunjes, VP of Digital Services • Jerry Bennington, VP of New Product Development

Facebook: facebook.com/idwpublishing • Twitter: @idwpublishing • YouTube: youtube.com/idwpublishing
Tumblr: tumblr.idwpublishing.com • Instagram: instagram.com/idwpublishing

Originally published as UNCLE SCROOGE issues #20–22 (Legacy #424–426).

The Roundabout Rally

From Brazilian *O Pato Donald* #992, 1970
Writer: Dick Kinney
Artist: Tony Strobl
Inker: Steve Steere
Colorist: Digikore Studios
Letterer: Jesse Post
Translation: David Gerstein
Dialogue: David Gerstein and Joe Torcivia

The Golden Birds

From Italian *Disney Anni D'Oro* #5, 2009
Writer and Artist: Romano Scarpa and Luca Boschi
Inker: Sandro Del Conte
Colorists: Disney Italia with Digikore Studios
Letterers: Nicole and Travis Seitler with Romano Scarpa
Translation and Dialogue: Thad Komorowski

Going Medieval

From Danish *Anders And & Co.* #39-40/2003
Writer: Gorm Transgaard
Artist: Victor "Vicar" Arriagada Rios
Colorist: Digikore Studios
Letterers: Nicole and Travis Seitler
Translation and Dialogue: Joe Torcivia

Obedience

From Swedish *Kalle Anka & C:o* #12/2012
Writer: Kai Vainiomäki
Artist: Carlos Mota
Colorists: Digikore Studios
Letterers: Nicole and Travis Seitler
Dialogue: Byron Erickson

Series Editor: Sarah Gaydos
Archival Editor: David Gerstein

Cover Artist: Andrea Freccero
Cover Colorist: Mario Perrotta
Collection Editors: Justin Eisinger
and Alonzo Simon
Collection Designer: Clyde Grapa
Publisher: Ted Adams

Art by Andrea Freccero, Colors by Mario Perrotta

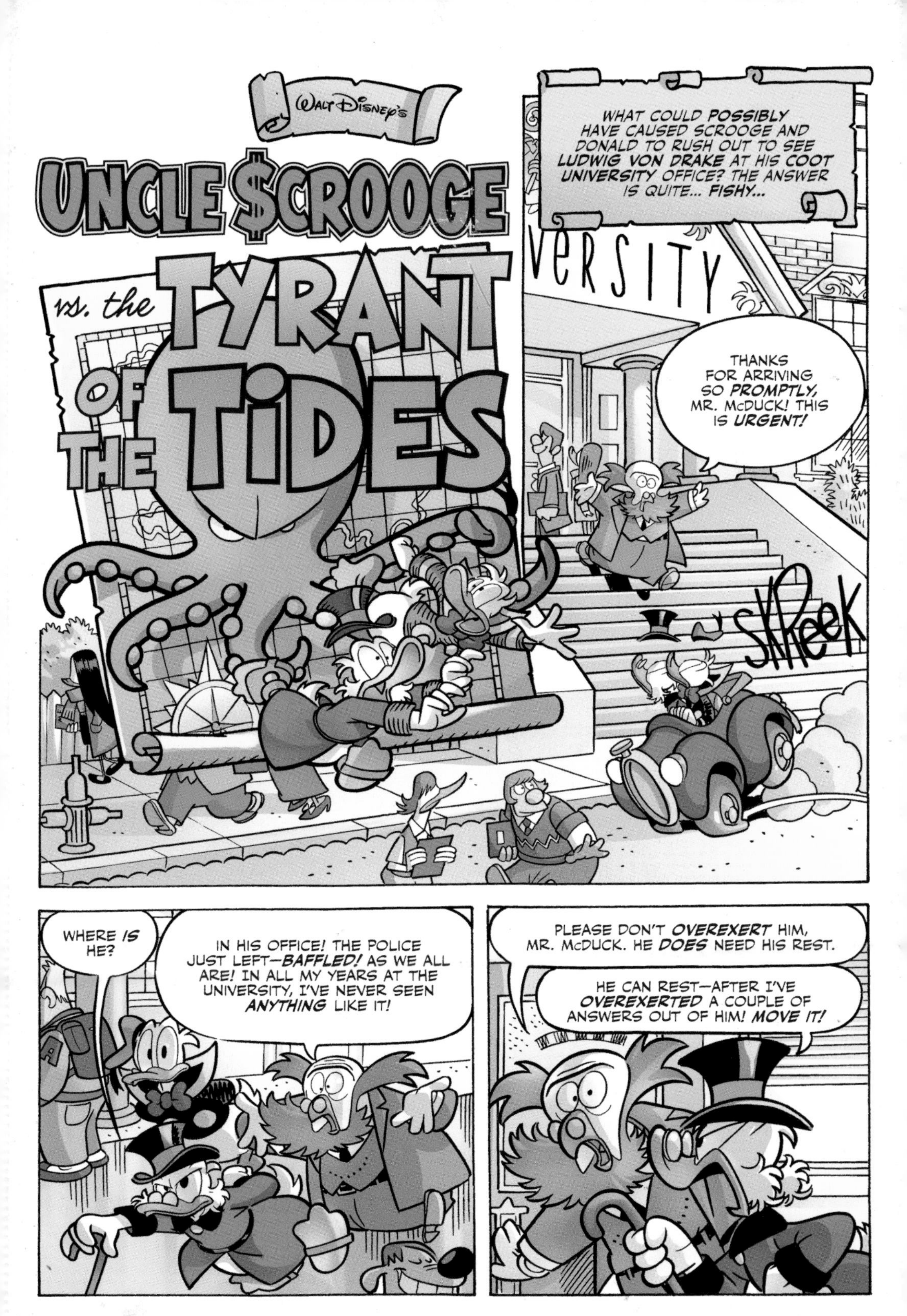

Originally published in *Topolino* #3000 (Italy, 2013)

LUDWIG, OLD BOY! WHAT HAPPENED!?
HO-HO! SCROOGE! COME, COME! THERE IS SOMETHING I HAVE TO TELL YOU!
AND THEN SOME.

WHAT IS IT? WHAT AILS YOU?
LISTEN WELL...
HOW DO YOU KNOW A MARINE PROFESSOR HAS LOST IT? WHEN HE FLUNKS A RIVER FOR RUNNING ITS COURSE!

HO-HO-HO-HO-HO!
!
ZIP
SMACK

WHAT DO YOU MEAN BY THAT?
UNCLE LUDWIG MADE AN ABOVE-AVERAGE JOKE! STOP THE PRESSES, THIS IS SERIOUS.
HO-HO-HO-HO-HO!

DEAN O'BRAIN! I DEMAND AN EXPLANATION!
GLADLY! PROFESSOR VON DRAKE WAS ATTACKED AND ROBBED LAST NIGHT! BY WHO WE DON'T KNOW, BUT THE ASSAILANT LEFT A CALLING CARD...

...WITH A MESSAGE ON THE BACK FOR *YOU!*

LET'S SEE... *"LAST WARNING! KEEP OUT OF THE OCEAN! THE SEA BELONGS TO THE SEA!"*
SIGNED... ***"TYRANT OF THE TIDES!"*** HIM ***AGAIN!?***

HO-HO! A BIG SQUIDDY MEANIE WITH A STRANGE WEAPON BARGED IN... AND ***ZAP!*** MY HEAD IS ***CRYSTAL CLEAR!*** BY THE WAY, WHY IS A RAVEN LIKE A WRITING DESK?

WHAT PROFESSOR VON DRAKE ***MEANS*** IS THAT'S ALL HE CAN ***REMEMBER!***
AND ALL OF THE RESEARCH ON HIS DESK WAS STOLEN!

THIS MAY BE THE ***END*** OF ***OPERATION: 3,000 LEAGUES,*** MR. McDUCK!
WAIT! ***THERE'S MORE!*** THE THIEF SAID HE WAS LOOKING FOR ***MONEY*** IN MY OFFICE... SO. I HELPED HIM! PFFTH...

HO-HO-HO-HO-HO!
BAM
BAM
BAM
...AND... ***HIM?***

DR. HÜBERMAIER IS THE UNIVERSITY'S MEDICINAL LUMINARY... AND THE DIAGNOSIS IS NOT ENCOURAGING!
INDEED! OUR COLLEAGUE HAS A CLEAR CASE OF BONKUS-OF-THE-KONKUS!
SKRNCH
SKRNCH

IN SUMMATION: HIS ENCYCLOPEDIC KNOWLEDGE HAS VANISHED INTO THIN AIR—FOR A WHILE! A LITTLE REST AND HE'LL RETURN TO NORMAL!
THAT'S THE GOOD NEWS! I ADVISE YOU TO KEEP PROFESSOR VON DRAKE OUT OF YOUR ADVENTURE, MR. McDUCK!

AND I ADVISE YOU TO KEEP YOUR BEAK OUT OF MY BUSINESS! OPERATION: 3,000 LEAGUES WILL GO FORWARD... AND LUDWIG IS COMING WITH ME!
!

THE SEA AIR WILL PUT HIM IN ORDER! COME, LUDWIG... YOU TOO, DONALD! PACK YOUR BAGS! IT'S SAILIN' TIME!
SAILIN' WHERE? YOU BARK AT ME TO DRIVE YOU OVER HERE AT THE SPEED OF LIGHT...

...BUT I AIN'T TAKIN' ANOTHER STEP TILL I KNOW WHERE I'M A-STEPPIN'! I HAVE NO INTEREST IN TANGLING WITH A MONSTER CARRYING A ZAPGUN AND TERRIFYING BUSINESS CARDS!
FINE! IF YOU MUST KNOW...

DID YOU EVER HEAR ABOUT THE SUBMARINE NAUTILUS? NOT THE SHIP JULES VERNE INVENTED FOR CAPTAIN NEMO IN HIS BOOKS... THE REAL ONE!
A REAL NAUTILUS? YOU'RE KIDDING!

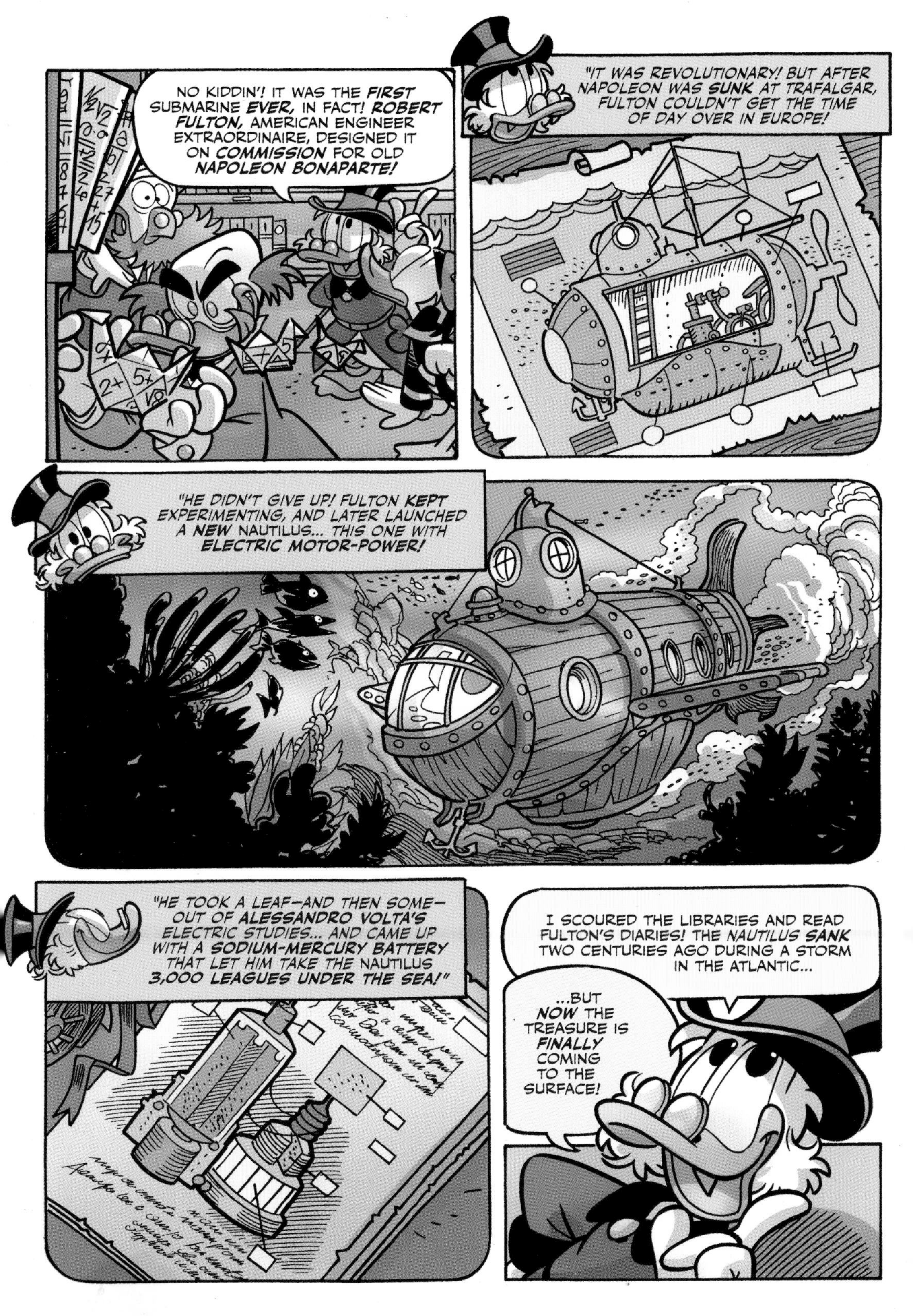
NO KIDDIN'! IT WAS THE FIRST SUBMARINE EVER, IN FACT! ROBERT FULTON, AMERICAN ENGINEER EXTRAORDINAIRE, DESIGNED IT ON COMMISSION FOR OLD NAPOLEON BONAPARTE!
"IT WAS REVOLUTIONARY! BUT AFTER NAPOLEON WAS SUNK AT TRAFALGAR, FULTON COULDN'T GET THE TIME OF DAY OVER IN EUROPE!
"HE DIDN'T GIVE UP! FULTON KEPT EXPERIMENTING, AND LATER LAUNCHED A NEW NAUTILUS... THIS ONE WITH ELECTRIC MOTOR-POWER!
"HE TOOK A LEAF—AND THEN SOME—OUT OF ALESSANDRO VOLTA'S ELECTRIC STUDIES... AND CAME UP WITH A SODIUM-MERCURY BATTERY THAT LET HIM TAKE THE NAUTILUS 3,000 LEAGUES UNDER THE SEA!"
I SCOURED THE LIBRARIES AND READ FULTON'S DIARIES! THE NAUTILUS SANK TWO CENTURIES AGO DURING A STORM IN THE ATLANTIC...
...BUT NOW THE TREASURE IS FINALLY COMING TO THE SURFACE!

WHAT TREASURE?
THE BATTERY, NEPHEW! IT'LL CHANGE THE FUTURE OF TRANSPORTATION!

AND EVER SINCE I'VE BEEN ON THE TRAIL OF THE NAUTILUS, I'VE BEEN GETTING EMPTY THREATS FROM THIS "TYRANT OF THE TIDES" LUG!

BUT THAT SQUID-JERK'S BULLYING WON'T STOP ME! SCROOGE McDUCK DIDN'T BECOME SCROOGE McDUCK BY BEING A COWARD!
BUT THE TYRANT STOLE FULTON'S DIARIES AND PROFESSOR VON DRAKE'S NOTES!
JUNK

I WASN'T BORN YESTERDAY! I HAVE COPIES OF EVERYTHING, INCLUDING LUDWIG'S NOTES! OPERATION: 3,000 LEAGUES WILL GO ON!

NICE ADVANTAGE, UNCLE SCROOGE! SO THIS TIDES TYRANT WILL THINK YOU'LL HAVE TO CALL IT QUITS...
WHEN WE'VE REALLY SET OFF IMMEDIATELY TO SEARCH FOR THE WRECK OF THE NAUTILUS! C'MON, LUDWIG, WE'LL TAKE CARE OF YOU!

WHO, ME? OH, NO! I'VE GOT A BELLY-ACHE!
SEE? PERFECTLY SANE. WITH A LITTLE OCEAN SCENERY, YOU'LL BE BACK TO THE OLD VON DRAKE IN NO TIME! AND IF NOT, THERE'S ALWAYS OLD-FASHIONED, FRUGAL SHOCK THERAPY...

AND SO, AFTER A COAST-TO-COAST FLIGHT, THE THREE DUCKS SET SAIL ON THE ATLANTIC OCEAN...
WAIT! ANOTHER DISCOVERY! ACCORDING TO MY CALCULATIONS... APPROXIMATELY 3.14% OF ALL SAILORS... ARE PI-RATES.

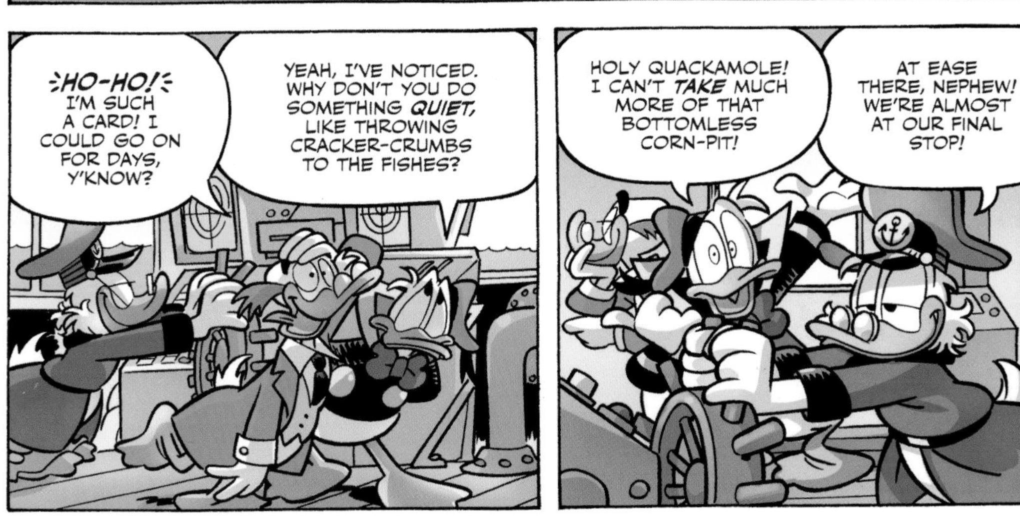
HO-HO! I'M SUCH A CARD! I COULD GO ON FOR DAYS, Y'KNOW?
YEAH, I'VE NOTICED. WHY DON'T YOU DO SOMETHING QUIET, LIKE THROWING CRACKER-CRUMBS TO THE FISHES?
HOLY QUACKAMOLE! I CAN'T TAKE MUCH MORE OF THAT BOTTOMLESS CORN-PIT!
AT EASE THERE, NEPHEW! WE'RE ALMOST AT OUR FINAL STOP!

ACCORDING TO FULTON'S DIARIES, THE NAUTILUS SUNK SOMEWHERE AROUND THE AZORES ISLANDS! ONCE WE ARRIVE, WE'LL SCOUR THE SEABED...

PARDON ME, SAIL-MATES!... HO-HO! ANYBODY GOT A CAN OPENER I CAN LOAN TO THE FISH?
LOAN... TO...?

THE FISH, SILLY BOY! THEY'LL NEED A CAN OPENER TO TASTE THOSE DELICIOUS BBQ BOSTON BAKED BEANS!
WAK! I SAID CRACKER-CRUMBS, YOU NINNY! THERE GOES OUR FOOD SUPPLY! WHAT WERE YOU THINKING!?

ACH! I DON'T THINK, DONALD, I ACT! NO CRACKERS IN THE PANTRY—IF I DIDN'T THROW THE CANS, THE FISH WOULD STARVE!
BUT NOW WE'LL STARVE!

OH, NO WE WON'T! WE'LL ADAPT TO OUR SURROUNDINGS LIKE I DID IN THE KLONDIKE! MUNCHING ALGAE AND DRINKING BOILED SEAWATER!
THIS AIN'T THE KLONDIKE! AND DON'T SAY WE!

WELL, I'M NOT WASTING TIME TURNING AROUND FOR MORE SUPPLIES! FORGET THE BEANS—WE'LL FEAST ON CRACKERS!
I'M SURE THERE'S A BOX SOMEWHERE IN MY CABIN!

EEEEK!
CRACKERS
DONNY, DON'T SHOUT! YOU'LL SCARE THE FISHES!
SHAKE
SHAKE

-AUGGH!- STRANDED, FOODLESS WITH AN ABSENT-MINDED PROFESSOR! YOUR BATTERY WILL LEAD US TO RUIN!
WRONG AGAIN, DONALD! THE BATTERY WILL LEAD ME TO FURTHER EXCESSIVE WEALTH!
ZIP

KNOW WHAT 3,000 LEAGUES COME TO? OVER 10,000 MILES! AND THE NAUTILUS MADE THAT LENGTH WITHOUT STOPPING FOR A SINGLE RECHARGE!

SO WHAT?
MY DEAR MYOPIC NEPHEW, CAN'T YOU SEE THE OBVIOUS? FULTON'S ELECTRIC MOTOR WILL BE THE ENGINE OF THE FUTURE! AND THE TYRANT OF THE TIDES KNOWS IT!

YOU SHOULD TAKE THAT GUY MORE SERIOUSLY! LOOK AT THE STATE HE LEFT UNCLE LUDWIG IN!
BAH! HE'S JUST LOOKING FOR A CASH GRAB, LIKE ALL MY RIVALS... THE ONLY DIFFERENCE IS HIS PENCHANT FOR SCREWBALL THEATRICS!

BEHIND EVERY TYRANT'S MASK IS A WANNABE LIKE ROCKERDUCK OR GLOMGOLD! AND SCROOGE McDUCK LAYS WASTE TO ALL OF 'EM! NOTHING TO WORRY ABOUT...
FOR YOU, ANYWAY!

AYE! BUT HEAR MY PLANS FOR THE NEXT McDUCK INNOVATION! THE AUTO INDUSTRY HAS BEEN TINKERING WITH ELECTRIC MOTORS FOR SOME TIME...

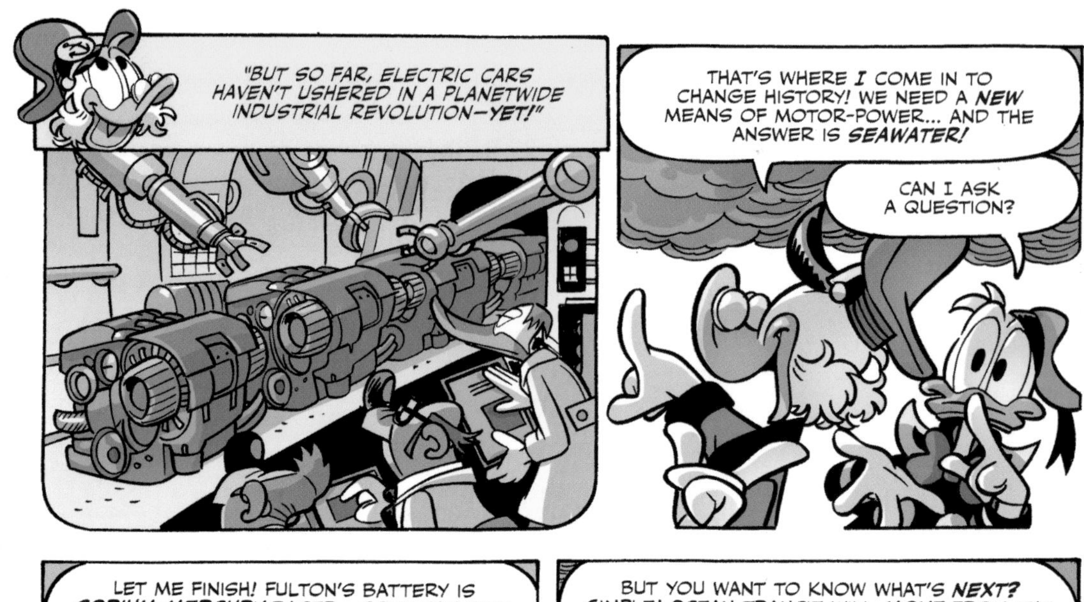
"BUT SO FAR, ELECTRIC CARS HAVEN'T USHERED IN A PLANETWIDE INDUSTRIAL REVOLUTION—YET!"
THAT'S WHERE I COME IN TO CHANGE HISTORY! WE NEED A NEW MEANS OF MOTOR-POWER... AND THE ANSWER IS SEAWATER!
CAN I ASK A QUESTION?

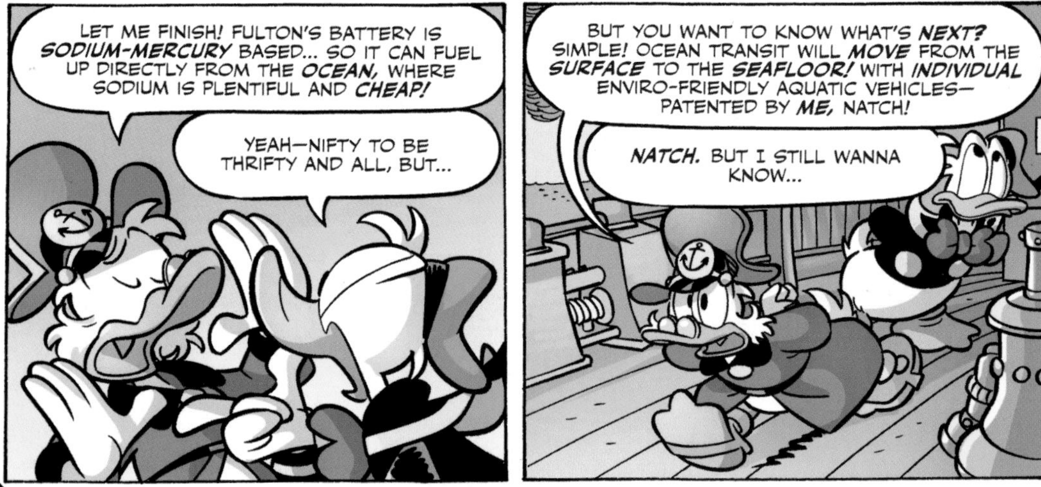
LET ME FINISH! FULTON'S BATTERY IS SODIUM-MERCURY BASED... SO IT CAN FUEL UP DIRECTLY FROM THE OCEAN, WHERE SODIUM IS PLENTIFUL AND CHEAP!
YEAH—NIFTY TO BE THRIFTY AND ALL, BUT...
BUT YOU WANT TO KNOW WHAT'S NEXT? SIMPLE! OCEAN TRANSIT WILL MOVE FROM THE SURFACE TO THE SEAFLOOR! WITH INDIVIDUAL ENVIRO-FRIENDLY AQUATIC VEHICLES—PATENTED BY ME, NATCH!
NATCH. BUT I STILL WANNA KNOW...

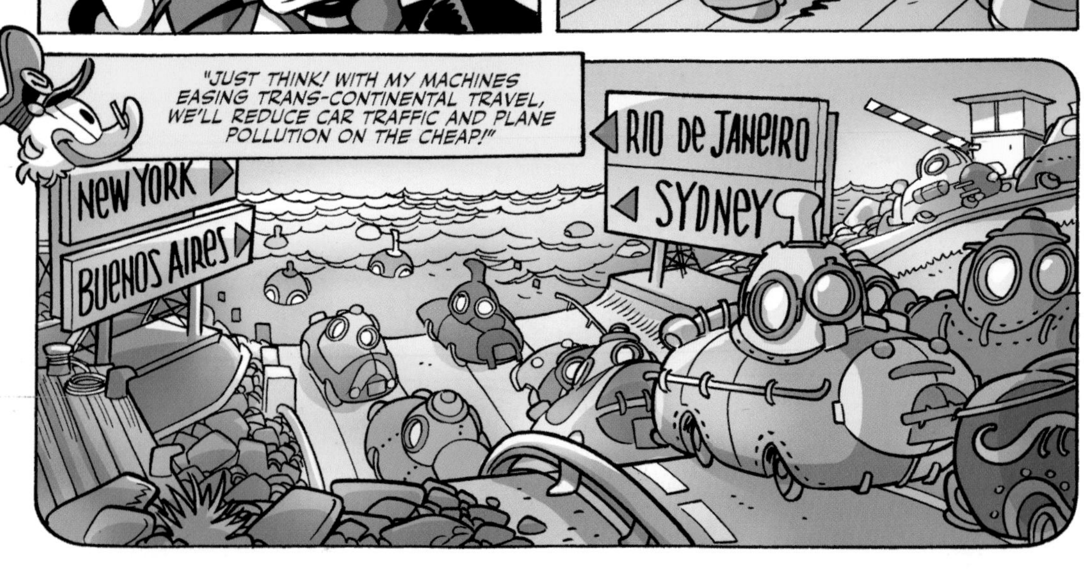
"JUST THINK! WITH MY MACHINES EASING TRANS-CONTINENTAL TRAVEL, WE'LL REDUCE CAR TRAFFIC AND PLANE POLLUTION ON THE CHEAP!"
NEW YORK
BUENOS AIRES
RIO DE JANEIRO
SYDNEY

"LOOK AT THE FIGURES! 71 PERCENT OF THE EARTH IS COVERED IN WATER... KNOW HOW MUCH **UNUTILIZED REAL ESTATE** THAT IS!? NEPHEW, THIS IS THE BEGINNING OF A **NEW ERA!**
"I CAN SEE IT NOW! FIRST UNDERSEA MOTORWAY **SHOPS** AND **HOTELS**... LATER, WHOLE **CITIES!** THE POSSIBILITIES ARE **ENDLESS!**"
McDUCK STATION
McDUCK STATION

AND IT'LL ALL BE THANKS TO SCROOGE McDUCK! ANY QUESTIONS, DONALD?
YEAH. WHO'S AT THE HELM?

KREEEEENNK

I HAD THE DARN SHIP SET ON AUTOPILOT! WHY HAS IT REVERSED COURSE!?
BROOOOOMM
PERHAPS THE AUTOPILOT IS MORE SENSIBLE THAN YOU!

OR MAYBE SOMEONE ELSE HAS TAKEN THE HELM! LUDWIG!
I AM THE CAPTAIN OF AN OLD EYESORE, AND A RIGHT GOOD CAPTAIN... HOO-HOO! SO GIVE THREE CHEERS AND THREE CHEERS MORE, FOR CAPTAIN LUDWIG OF THE OLD EYESORE!
WHRRRRR

WHAT'S WITH THE SAILOR GET-UP?
AH, I BROUGHT IT FOR THE OCCASION! A PROFESSOR'S LIFE IS SO BORING—AND I ALWAYS DREAMED OF BEING A PIRATE! BLOODTHIRSTY ADVENTURE, EXCITING STORMS...

...OH, SPEAKING OF WHICH, BY THE WAY...

KRA-KOOM
AUGGGH!
SNORT!

BAW! WE'RE THROUGH! ALL WASHED UP!
BAH! WE'VE FACED WORSE! IT'S A DILLY OF A STORM, BUT I DIDN'T BECOME SCROOGE McDUCK BY DELAYING TRIPS ON ACCOUNT OF A LITTLE RAIN, OR SLEET, OR SNOW...

NO MORE STORIES! I WANNA GO HOME! UNCLE LUDWIG, LET'S SCOOT! MAN THE LIFEBOATS!

SPLASH

LOWERED THE LIFEBOATS, MY CAPTAIN! HOO-HOO!
OH, GIVE ME STRENGTH.

SKRA-DOOM

WELL, LOOK WHO'S BACK! I THOUGHT YOU'D BE DRYING OFF IN DUCKBURG BY NOW!
THE PROFESSOR MADE ANOTHER MISCALCULATION. WE'VE LOST OUR RAFTS! C'MON, UNCLE SCROOGE, LET'S GO HOME! IT'S TOO DANGEROUS TO KEEP ON FULTON'S TRAIL!

HIS WRECK'S BEEN WAITING FOR CENTURIES! ONE MORE DAY WON'T MAKE A DIFFERENCE! MAYBE YOU'LL BE WASTING YOUR TIME... BUT THINK OF US!
AND LET SOMEONE ELSE GET HIS CLUTCHES ON THE NAUTILUS BEFORE ME? BAH!

THIS STORM WON'T LAST FOREVER! I FACED WORSE TRAPPING CRABS UP IN VANCOUVER! DID I EVER TELL YOU ABOUT THOSE DAYS...?
NO, BUT I EXPECT A RIVETING ACCOUNT!

SEVERAL HOURS OF CRAB STORIES LATER—THE SKY IS CLEAR!
GOOD NEWS, MEN! THE UGLY WEATHER'S WELL BEHIND US...

...AND WE'VE REACHED OUR DESTINATION! THAT WASN'T SO BAD, EH?
GROAN! YEAH, A CAKE-WALK!

LUDWIG, OLD BOY, HOW DO YOU FEEL? YOUR BONKUS-OF-THE-KONKUS UN-BONKED? GET YOUR MEMORY BACK? QUICK, WHAT'S EIGHT TIMES EIGHT?
DONKEY MEAT!
EXCELLENT! SPLENDID, EVEN!

EVERYONE ABOARD THE BATHYSPHERE! MY SONAR SHOWS SOMETHING *INTRIGUING* RIGHT BELOW US! WE'RE SCOURING THE SEABED!
I'LL STAY HERE, THANKS! I'VE HAD ENOUGH ADVENTURE FOR TODAY!

OH, DON'T BE *RIDICULOUS. GET IN!*
!
PAFF

*"YOU CAN **NEVER** HAVE ENOUGH ADVENTURE!"*

WE'VE DETECTED SOMETHING THAT *COULD* BE THE WRECK OF THE *NAUTILUS!* MODERN TECHNOLOGY IS ANNOYINGLY *PRICEY...* BUT IT MAKES TREASURE HUNTING A BREEZE!
I'M BORED! ISN'T ANYTHING ELSE ON? WE GET *LOTSA* DIFFERENT STATIONS AT HOME! EVEN A 24-HOUR PUDDING CHANNEL!

HERE, IT'S *MY TURN* TO PICK A SHOW! AND COULD I ALSO HAVE A SLICE OF CINNAMON TOAST? AND A CUP OF COFFEE, A SANDWICH, AND YOO-OU...
HEY! WHAT'S THE IDEA!? STOP THAT! DON'T TOUCH—
BZZZ
KRRRR
CLIK CLIK...

YAUUUUUGH!
VRRRRRRRR

ZONK

PUT THE HEADLIGHTS ON, UNCLE SCROOGE! I CAN'T SEE WHERE WE ARE...

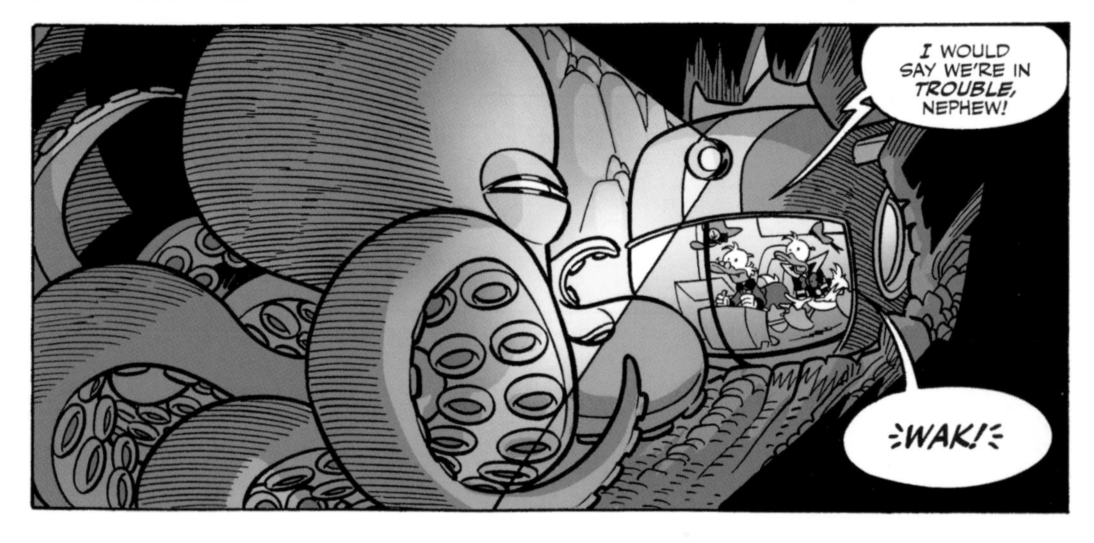
I WOULD SAY WE'RE IN TROUBLE, NEPHEW!
WAK!

HOW MANY TICKLES DOES IT TAKE TO MAKE AN OCTOPUS LAUGH? TEN-TICKLES!
VRRRRRRRRRRRRRRR
SHUT UP, LUDWIG.

FASTER, UNCLE SCROOGE! FASTER!
I'VE ALMOST GOT US OUT OF HERE! JUST A BIT MORE...

...WE'RE SAFE!
FSSHH

OR MAYBE NOT!

AVAST THERE, McDUCK! SHOULDA HEEDED MY WARNINGS! NOW YOU'LL FACE THE *TYRANT OF THE TIDES' WRATH!* GET ONBOARD!
WAK! IT'S YOUR CASH-GRABBING WANNABE, UNCLE SCROOGE!
POK

GULP! NO OFFENSE, MR. TYRANT! WE WERE JUST TAKING UNCLE LUDWIG OUT FOR SOME FRESH SALTY AIR...
SHADDAP! YOU *CHALLENGED* THE SEA—NOW YOU WILL BE *PUNISHED!* MY SPECIAL ZAP-GUN WILL *WIPE YOUR MINDS...* AND THEN YOU'LL BE LEFT TO *FATE!*

THE SEA AND I WILL *DECIDE* WHETHER TO BE MERCIFUL... *IF* YOU'RE WILLING TO PLEAD FOR MY PARDON!
SEEMS LIKE A SQUARE DEAL. SCROOGE McDUCK *ALWAYS* MAKES IT SQUARE...

...BUT *HIS WAY!* HOW'S THIS FOR A *COUNTER-OFFER,* OCTO-PUSS?
ZING
POK

TSK! YOU MADE YOUR *GUN* OUT OF *GOLD?* ANY *IDIOT* COULD TELL YOU *STEEL* IS WORTH *MORE* IN THIS CASE!
BLARGH!
CRASH

STAY WHERE Y' ARE, DUCK! DROP THE SWORD OR I'LL SHOOT!
GRUNT! NO CALAMARI IS GONNA PUSH *US* AROUND!

OOF!
HA! NICELY DONE, DONALD! I CAN *ALWAYS* COUNT ON YOU—WHEN IT *COUNTS!*
BUMP
ZIP

KEEP 'EM COVERED! I WANT A CLOSER LOOK AT THIS *"TYRANT!"*
AWRIGHT, AWRIGHT!

DEAN O'BRAIN!?
GROAN!

AND GET A LOAD OF *THESE* BEAUTY BOYS!
DR. HÜBERMAIER! PROFESSOR COOPER! BUT... WHAT DOES THIS *MEAN!?*

SIGH! THE JIG IS UP, MY FRIENDS! THERE WAS NO THEFT, OR MEMORY LOSS! IT WAS ALL *MY* MASTER STRATEGY... AND IT MASTERFULLY WENT *KABLOOEY!*
LUDWIG! I DON'T UNDERSTAND! IS THIS A JOKE...?

NO JOKE, SCROOGEY-BOY! THERE NEVER WAS A "TYRANT OF THE TIDES"... BUT WE PUT OUR PLAN INTO ACTION SO YOU WOULDN'T BECOME THAT TYRANT!
SNORT! SO THIS CHARADE WAS JUST TO SNAFU THE WHOLE WORKS, EH? I'M FLATTERED!

I HAVE NEVER DENIED YOU ACCESS TO MY BRILLIANT MIND, BUT THIS TIME YOUR PLAN WAS JUST PLAIN DANGEROUS!
PROFESSOR VON DRAKE TOLD US ABOUT IT AS SOON AS YOU GOT ON THE NAUTILUS' TRAIL!

ACH! FULTON'S ELECTRIC MOTOR WAS A BRILLIANT INVENTION, FOR SURE... BUT AN UNDERSEA HIGHWAY AND WORLD IS JUST PLAIN SCARY!
HUMANITY JUST ISN'T READY FOR IT, MR. McDUCK!

SO IT'S UP TO YOU EGGHEADS TO DECIDE WHAT'S RIGHT AND WRONG FOR HUMANITY? I LIKE THAT! SNARL!
THINK, SCROOGE! EVERY DAY MANKIND ALREADY DOES GREAT DAMAGE TO THE SEA... WITH LIMITED ACCESS, YET!

YOUR INTENTIONS ARE HONEST, BUT THE RISK OF CATASTROPHE IS JUST AROUND THE CORNER!
SO YOU WANT TO STOP SCIENTIFIC PROGRESS?

IT SEEMS KOOKY FOR THIS TO COME OUT OF LUDWIG VON DRAKE'S MOUTH... BUT IF YOU CARE ABOUT THE WORLD WE LIVE IN—YES!

YOU KNOW WHAT, GENTLEMEN? YOU'VE CONVINCED ME TO STOP!
REALLY?

AYE! YOU'VE CONVINCED ME TO STOP... GIVING GENEROUS DONATIONS TO COOT UNIVERSITY! SAY GOODBYE TO YOUR FREE RIDES, YOU INTERFERING KNOW-IT-ALLS!
BUT UNCLE SCROOGE! THE UNIVERSITY NEEDS YOUR MONEY TO SURVIVE!

ER—NOT QUITE! MR. McDUCK'S "DONATION" IS SUPPLYING THE STUDENT CAFETERIA WITH PIZZA!
DELICIOUS PIZZA! EVERYONE FROM CALISOTA TO ALASKA GOES CRAZY FOR SCROOGISSIMO PIES™!
CRAZY IS RIGHT! THEY TASTE LIKE WORN-OUT BARSTOOLS!
THEY'RE MADE FROM RECYCLED WORN-OUT BARSTOOLS—AND WHY NOT? KIDS LOVE 'EM!

OPERATION: 3,000 LEAGUES WILL GO ON—WITH OR WITHOUT YOU! YOU THOUGHT YOUR AMATEUR THEATRICS WOULD SCARE ME?

THREATENING LETTERS! TOY GUNS! COSTUMES! BAH! BUT I'LL ADMIT, LUDWIG... YOU PLAYED YOUR PART OF THE INSANE WALKING HINDRANCE WELL!
THANK YOU! AMONGST MY ACCOMPLISHMENTS IS AN M.A. IN THEATRICAL IDIOCY! COULDN'T UNDERSTAND A WORD MY FACULTY ADVISER SAID, POOR BOY...

BUT ALAS! I TRIED EVERYTHING TO HINDER YOUR QUEST—AND FAILED!
INDEED! LET'S GO, DONALD! THE NAUTILUS AWAITS!

NO.
!!

NO?! WHADDAYA MEAN, "NO"?!
AH, LET ME EXPLAIN! IT'S AN ADVERB THAT INDICATES DISSENT, DENIAL, OR REFUSAL! ITS ORIGINS DATE BACK TO OLD ENGLISH OF THE 13TH CENTURY—

I KNOW WHAT "NO" MEANS, VON DORK! I WANNA KNOW WHAT HE MEANS BY SAYING IT!
IT MEANS THAT I WILL NOT BE PARTICIPATING IN THIS GREEDY ENDEAVOR! UNCLE LUDWIG IS RIGHT!

YOUR IDEA IS FANTASTIC, BUT IT'S *DANGEROUS!* SUBMARINE TRAFFIC WOULD DISRUPT SEA LIFE, AND...
SPARE THE MISER-SHAMING, DONALD! I SUB ALONE! I DON'T NEED *ANY* OF YOU!

BUT UNK...
GO HOME, *EX-NEPHEW!* I'LL RECOVER THE BATTERY FROM THE *NAUTILUS MYSELF!*

AND IF YOU DON'T LIKE IT, JUST *TRY* TO STOP ME!

COURAGE, DONNY...

"SCROOGE McDUCK DIDN'T BECOME SCROOGE McDUCK BY LISTENING TO OTHERS!"
VRRRRRRRRRRRR

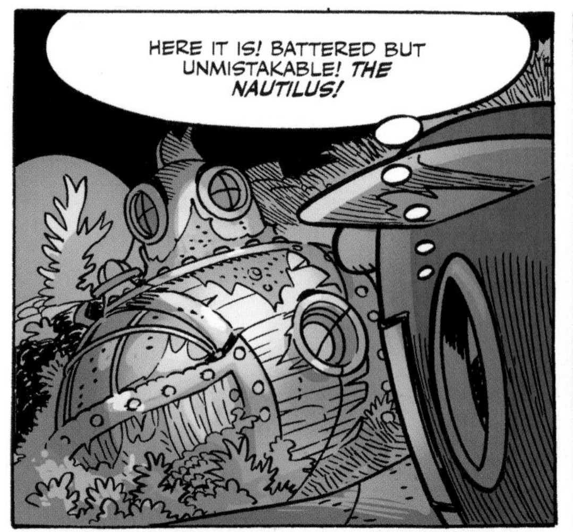
HERE IT IS! BATTERED BUT UNMISTAKABLE! *THE NAUTILUS!*

I FEEL JUST LIKE A KID AT CHRISTMAS! THERE'S MY PRESENT UNDER THE TREE—AND I CAN'T WAIT TO *UNWRAP IT!*

SKRANG

EUREKA!

FULTON'S BATTERY! FULLY CHARGED AND READY TO RUN!

EH? WHAT'S THIS NOW...?
SWIP

BURST ME BAGPIPES! THE GIANT OCTOPUS—AGAIN! THAT RUDE AWAKENING MUST HAVE PUT HER IN A REALLY BAD MOOD!

THIS DOES NOT BODE WELL! THE BATHYSPHERE CAN WITHSTAND THE PRESSURE OF THE DEEP—BUT I DIDN'T HAVE IT TESTED FOR TENTACLE PRESSURE!
I NEED REINFORCEMENT!

HEY UP THERE! ANYONE THERE!? THIS IS SCROOGE! MAYDAY! NEED HELP! OCTOPUS! HELP!
!

SCROOGE IS IN TROUBLE! QUICK, GET HIS POSITION, COOPER!
FZZZZ.... DO YOU READ ME? TRAPPED ON THE SEABED.... BZZZKK... NEED HELP... QUICK... FZZZ...

BZZZZZZZKKK...
LOST TRANSMISSION! THAT IS NOT A GOOD SIGN!

BLASTED TRANSMITTER'S BUSTED! STUPID BEAST MUST'VE WRECKED IT!
BZZZZZZZKKK...
CLICK
CLICK
CLICK

BDOOONG

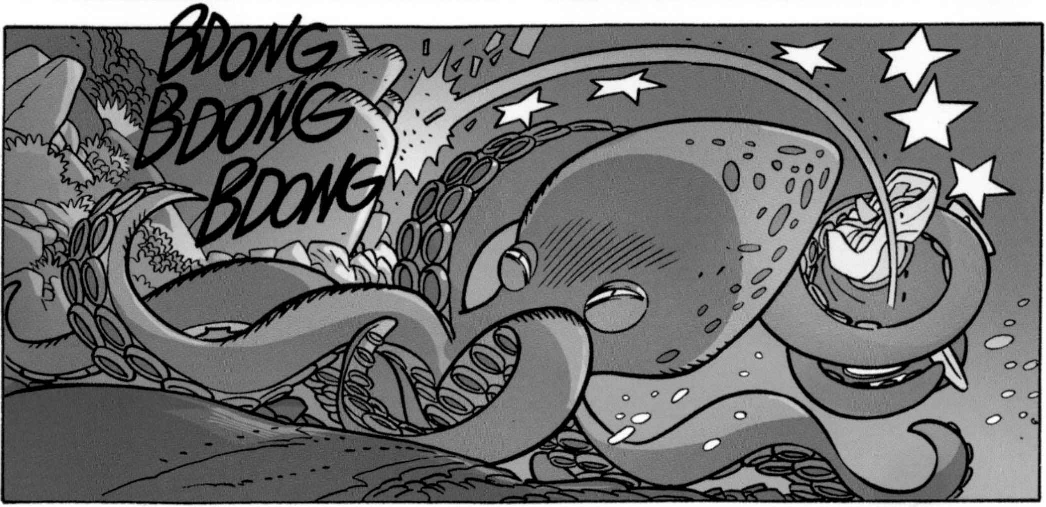
BDONG
BDONG
BDONG

WHAT'LL WE DO? WE DON'T HAVE ANOTHER BATHYSPHERE TO REACH UNCLE SCROOGE!
TRUE, DONALD! BUT—WITH FOUR BRILLIANT SCIENTIFIC MINDS ABOARD, WE CAN ALWAYS **MAKE** ONE!

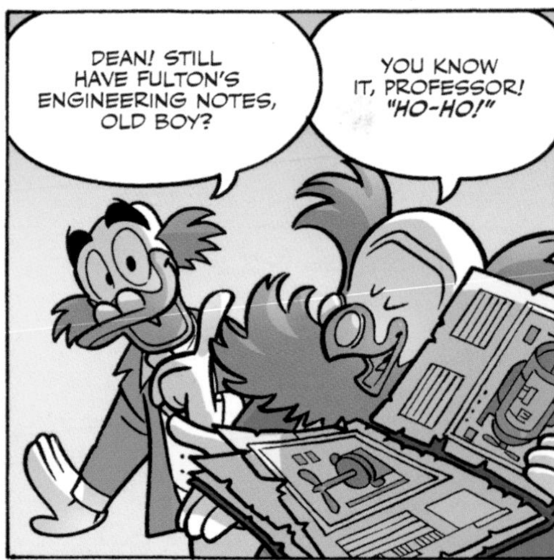
DEAN! STILL HAVE FULTON'S ENGINEERING NOTES, OLD BOY?
YOU KNOW IT, PROFESSOR! ***"HO-HO!"***

TOP SPEED THEN, MEN! WE'LL USE PARTS OF THIS SHIP TO BUILD A *MAKESHIFT RESCUE SUBMARINE!*
YOU HEARD HIM! GET THE PLIERS AND HAMMERS! FIRE UP THE BLOWTORCH!

KLONG

THIS SUB WAS GUARANTEED *UNSINKABLE!* AND I HAD TO GO AND THROW AWAY THE RECEIPT!
CRRRK

WHIMPER! DONALD WAS RIGHT... BUT WHAT GOOD IS REGRET WHEN IT'S TOO LATE?
CRRRK

BLUBLUBLUBLUBLBL
TARGET SIGHTED! FIRE UP THE ENGINES! *FULL SPEED AHEAD!*

"ENGINES," HE SAYS!
BRACE YOURSELVES, KIDS! WE'VE GOTTA STAGE A HECKUVA DIVERSION TO GET MS. OCTOPUS AWAY FROM SCROOGE!

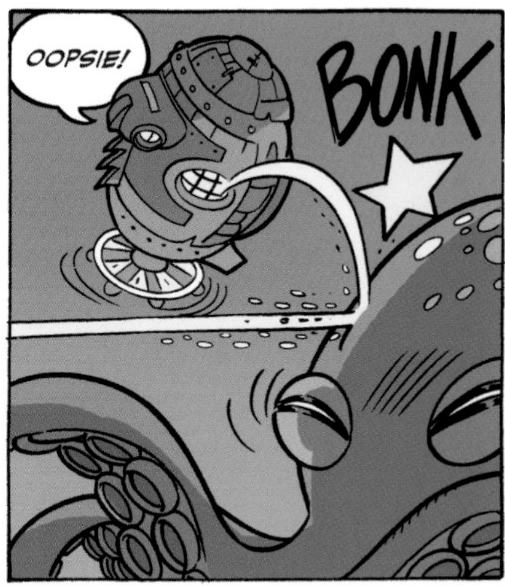
OOPSIE!
BONK

INGENIOUS PLAN, VON DRAKE. I DON'T KNOW HOW YOU DO IT.
FASTER! SO I GOOFED ON THE SPECIFICS! BUT IT STILL WORKED! FASTER! THE OCTOPUS LET GO OF SCROOGE!

BUT NOW SHE WANTS TO CRUSH US!
TUT-TUT! CEPHALOPODS ARE INTELLIGENT, BUT PREDICTABLE! CHARMING CREATURES, REALLY!
THOUGH YOU WOULDN'T WANT TO KISS ONE! HO-HO!

WE'RE HEADED RIGHT FOR THAT WRECK!
YEP! THE NAUTILUS—AND THE INFAMOUS SODIUM-MERCURY BATTERY! TWO HUNDRED YEARS SHOULD BE ENOUGH TIME FOR A FULL RECHARGE, EH?
POK

SO WHAT?
SO YOU BETTER SKEDADDLE ON MY SIGNAL, OR WE'RE ALL SUNK!

AND THAT, GENTLEMEN, IS WHY YOU NEVER HANDLE ELECTRICITY BARE-HANDED!
CRUNK
SHRAKAZAKK

WHOA! THAT WAS GREAT, UNCLE LUDWIG! THERE GOES THE OCTOPUS!
YES, AND HERE WE GO TO HAUL SCROOGE AND HIS BATHYSPHERE TO SAFETY... AND FINISH THIS DEEP SEA TOUR!

BACK ON DECK!
WE, THE ESTEEMED FACULTY OF COOT UNIVERSITY, JUST HAVE ONE THING TO SAY, MR. McDUCK: THANKS, MAN!
FOR WHAT? I'VE CAUSED YOU GENTS NOTHING BUT TROUBLE!

AU CONTRAIRE! I HAVEN'T FELT THIS ALIVE IN DECADES! THE THRILL—THE EXCITEMENT—ALL THANKS TO YOU!
HMM...

I SHOULD BE THANKING YOU... FOR MY LIFE. AND I'M PRETTY SURE I DON'T DESERVE THIS!
ACH, THINK NOTHING OF IT... THE BATTERY'S WHAT YOU WANTED, EH?

I DON'T THINK SO! YOU MADE YOUR POINT... AND SO DID THAT OCTOPUS! THE SEAFLOOR JUST ISN'T READY FOR HUMAN TRAVEL OR OCCUPATION!
"THE SEA BELONGS TO THE SEA"—TO QUOTE OUR FRIEND THE "TYRANT"!

A TYRANT I'D RATHER NOT BE REMEMBERED AS! FULTON'S BATTERY WILL BE USED STRICTLY FOR STUDY! BESIDES, WHO KNOWS WHERE IT'LL LEAD US?
YOU COULD ALWAYS REPLACE GASOLINE WITH SEAWATER!

HMMM... I LIKE THAT! THIS COULD BE THE START OF SOMETHING BIG—THE AQUA-MOTOR!
SO I TAKE IT I'M NO LONGER YOUR EX-NEPHEW, THEN?
ZIP

NOPE! REINSTATED! FOR THIS NEW ENDEAVOR, I NEED SOMEONE I CAN TRUST AT MY SIDE! THIS DREAM IS LEAGUES AWAY INDEED...

BUT WHEN SCROOGE McDUCK HAS A DREAM—AND HIS KIN!—NO NUMBER OF LEAGUES MAKE IT UNREACHABLE!
the End

WALT DISNEY'S

UNCLE RUMPUS

ASTRAY FOR A DAY

Originally published in *Aku Ankka* #23/2012 (Finland, 2012)

HUH! A VERY APPROPRIATE SIMILE, GIVEN THE SETTING!

BUT ALAS, BEFORE LONG RUMPUS IS ONCE AGAIN ON THE MOVE!
ZZZZ!

DEEPER AND DEEPER INTO THE WOODS HE GOES...
ZZZZZ!

...ONE HOUR, THEN TWO...
ZZZ!

...THEN, SUDDENLY-
SNORT! HUH? WHERE AM I? THIS CERTAINLY DOES NOT LOOK LIKE THE CAMP!

OH, WELL, I COULDN'T HAVE GONE FAR IN JUST A FEW MINUTES! IT'S PROBABLY ON THE OTHER SIDE OF THOSE TWO BIG TREES!

YOWP!

SPLASH

AAH! THIS IS THE BEST MY FEET HAVE FELT ALL DAY!

BUT ALAS, THIS ISN'T THE WAY BACK TO THAT IDIOT CAMP!

SO, I GUESS I'LL TRY GOING IN THE OPPOSITE DIRECTION!

HMM! THIS IS CERTAINLY A TANGLE! I FEEL LIKE A FLEA CAUGHT IN A BRILLO PAD!

OUCH! THERE'S NO WAY I COULD HAVE GOTTEN THROUGH THIS MESS WITHOUT WAKING UP!
OW!

NOW THE TRICK IS TO GET OUT OF HERE!

SOON-
HALLELUJAH! PUFF! PUFF! FREEDOM AT LAST! NOW TO GET BACK TO-

YOICKS!

HOOO!
ME, WHO ELSE?

HOOO!
ARE YOU HARD OF HEARING, OR JUST STUBBORN?

HOOOO!
YOU! WHO DO YOU- OH, THE HECK WITH IT! THIS COULD GO ON ALL NIGHT!

DUMB BIRD! AH, HEY! THIS APPEARS TO BE A PATH OF SOME SORT! MAYBE MY LUCK IS CHANGING!

MAYBE, BUT NOT FOR LONG-
WHOOSH
WHAT THE DICKENS?

OH, LOVELY! JUST WHAT I NEEDED, A WIND STORM! AND LISTEN TO THOSE TREES BANGING INTO ONE ANOTHER!
CLONK CLONK

NOTHING LIKE A BIT OF FRESH AIR AND A LITTLE ACTIVITY!

KARUMPH

WHOOPSIE DAISY! MAKE THAT A **LOT** OF ACTIVITY! THIS IS GETTING TO BE LIKE SOME KIND OF COMPUTER GAME!

SOON, THOUGH THE WIND ABATES AND RELATIVE CALM RETURNS!

PHEW! WHAT'S NEXT? AN EARTHQUAKE? A VOLCANO ERUPTING? ANOTHER RECESSION?

GROWL

UH, OH! I MAY BE HUNGRY, BUT THAT DEFINITELY ISN'T MY TUMMY TALKING!
SNORT

TIME TO PUT ON A BIT OF STEAM, EVEN IF MY FEET ARE READY TO FALL OFF!

WHERE ON EARTH IS THE CAMP? I'M BEGINNING TO COME TO THE CONCLUSION THAT I'M **LOST**!

IT MUST BE AROUND HERE SOMEPLACE!

STILL, AFTER MORE HOURS OF STUMBLING ABOUT, THERE'S NO SIGN OF THE CAMP! IN FACT, RUMPUS SEEMS TO HAVE COME FULL CIRCLE!
HOOOO!

OH, NO! WE'RE NOT GOING THROUGH **THAT** AGAIN!

I'VE GOT TROUBLES ENOUGH JUST BEING **LOST**!

IMAGINE! ME! **LOST**! OH, THAT THE FATES SHOULD FROWN SO UPON MY WONDROUS SELF!

WOE IS ME! WHATEVER AM I TO DO? I'M POOPED TO THE TENTH POWER!

I'VE GOT TO GET SOME **SLEEP**!

AND LO, THIS IS JUST THE SPOT TO DO IT! SHELTERED, COMFY AND SECURE!

WHAT MORE COULD A POOR LOST WANDERER ASK? UNLESS IT WERE TWO CUPS OF COFFEE, SIX FRIED EGGS AND A SIDE OF BACON!

AND SOON, RUMPUS IS ASLEEP!
ZZZZ

MINUTES PASS, AND THEN...
ZZZZ SNORT!

YES, RUMPUS BEGINS TO SLEEPWALK!
ZZZ

SLOWLY HE MAKES HIS WAY THROUGH RAVINES...
ZZZZZZZ

... UP HILLS AND THROUGH A DALE...
ZZZZ

...UNTIL FINALLY AS THE SUN BEGINS TO SET HE ARRIVES AT THE CAMP!
ZZ- SNORT! HUH? WELL PRAISE BE, I'M BACK!
YOU'RE BACK, ALL RIGHT! WHERE ON EARTH HAVE YOU BEEN?

BELIEVE ME, IF I KNEW THAT, I WOULDN'T HAVE BEEN THERE!

AND SO RUMPUS RETURNS AT LAST TO THE MONEY BIN, SOMEWHAT THE WORST FOR WEAR AND COMPLETELY **UNCURED!**
FUSS! FUME! GROWL! **GROWF!**

WHAT'S THE MATTER, BRO, LOSE A FEW TRILLION BUCKS WHILE I WAS AWAY?

NO! I'M **UPSET!**

WHY? JUST BECAUSE I'M BACK SO SOON?
NO, BECAUSE NOW **I'VE** BEGUN TO WALK IN **MY** SLEEP!

DO TELL! WELL, IF WE HAPPEN TO BUMP INTO EACH OTHER SOME NIGHT...
YES?

...I'LL WAVE MY HAT AT YOU, BRO! BELIEVE ME, IT'LL BE LIKE A BREATH OF **FRESH AIR!**

AND A LOT EASIER ON THE **FEET!**

End

Originally published in *Donald Julealbum* #4 (Norway, 2013)

THAT'S WHY I HAFTA BUY THE BIGGEST BIRD IN THE SHOP! AS IF I WASN'T SPENDING ENOUGH MONEY AT CHRISTMAS!

BUT DEAREST NEPHEW! IF I'D KNOWN THAT'S HOW YOU FELT, I WOULDN'T HAVE COME!
IT'S JUST...I MAKE ALL THE PREPARATIONS, AND YOU JUST SHOW UP HUNGRY! CAN YOU RECALL EVER HAVING MADE SOMEBODY ELSE HAPPY AT CHRISTMAS?

...DID I EVER MAKE SOMEBODY ELSE HAPPY AT CHRISTMAS?

I BELIEVE I MAY HAVE DONE THAT LONG AGO...

I WAS TWELVE YEARS OLD AND LIVING IN GLASGOW, BACK IN THE OLD COUNTRY* WITH MY FOLKS! I HAD TO SHINE SHOES FOR YEARS TO SAVE UP ENOUGH FOR A SKINNY NAG AND A CART!
ALL SO I COULD WORK TO FEED MYSELF AND MY FAMILY BY DIGGING PEAT OUTSIDE OF TOWN AND SELLING IT FOR FUEL!
COME ON, POPPY ME LASS! A WEE EFFORT NOW!
*SCOTLAND!

HOW ARE YE DOING FOR PEAT, MRS. MACATEER?
I HOPE YOU CAN COME BY WITH SOME MORE THIS FRIDAY, SCROOGE ME LAD!

AND A GOOD THING TOO, POPPY LASS, IF I AIM TO KEEP YOU IN HAY! LUCKILY, I'VE GOT A BIG WEEKLY ORDER FOR PEAT AT THE STRATHBUNGO HOUSE GIRLS' ORPHANAGE!

AND THERE IT IS!

GOOD MORNING, MR. JOLLY!
NO PEAT TODAY, YOUNG McDUCK! I'M SORRY, BUT WE'RE QUITE ALL RIGHT FOR PEAT!

NAE BOTHER, I'LL BE BACK NEXT WEDNESDAY!
MAKE THAT THE WEDNESDAY AFTER NEXT, WON'T YOU, LADDIE?

THAT'S PECULIAR! I KNOW HE CAN'T HAVE ENOUGH PEAT TO LAST THE WEEK!
SNIFFLE!

THAT SOUNDED LIKE A KID! BUT IT'S COMING FROM THAT BUNDLE OF CLOTH!
SOB!

I KNOW YOU! YOU'RE BRENDA AND YOU LIVE IN THE ORPHANAGE!
P-PLEASE DON'T TELL MR. JOLLY I WAS SAD!

WHY? WOULD HE GET WORRIED?
MAYBE... AND HE'S GOT TROUBLES ENOUGH!

IT'S NOT HIS FAULT WE'RE CHILLY AND HAVE TO WORK LONG HOURS! IT'S HIS MEAN LANDLORD, MR. MACMISER, WHO INSISTS ON IT!

NOTHING WRONG WITH WORK!
NOT THIS KIND! HOLD MY WOOL AND I'LL SHOW YOU!

BUT ARE BOYS ALLOWED INSIDE?
ONLY IN SPECIAL CIRCUMSTANCES!

YOU'RE LATE! AND WHO'S THAT?
SORRY, MISS CRAMM! THIS DELIVERYMAN FROM THE MACKNITTY WOOLEN MILL INSISTED ON CARRYING THE CLOTH!
GOOD MORNING, MA'AM!

SHOW HIM TO THE FACTORY HALL! THEN GET HIM OUT OF HERE AND RETURN TO YOUR SEWING!
THAT'S NO WAY TO TALK TO A KID!
CLICK

THIS IS WHERE THEY MAKE US WORK 14-HOUR DAYS...SEWING KILTS! MR. JOLLY SAYS THE MARKET IS DOWN, SO WE HAVE TO WORK EVER-LONGER HOURS!
THAT'S NO WAY TO TREAT A KID!

GATHER ROUND, GIRLS! I HAVE A SAD ANNOUNCEMENT TO MAKE!
CLAP CLAP
HUZZAH!!!
?!

A SAD ANNOUNCEMENT MAKES THEM CHEER?
AYE! THEY'VE BEEN SEWING FOR SIX STRAIGHT HOURS WITHOUT A BREAK!

I'M SORRY TO SAY THAT OUR LANDLORD, MR. MacMISER...
...HAS RAISED THE RENT AGAIN!

B-BUT... HOW DID YOU KNOW?
WE MAY BE CHILDREN, MR. JOLLY, BUT WE ARE NOT FOOLS!
THE RENT HAS GONE UP THRICE SINCE AUGUST!

AND SINCE THE MARKET FOR OUR KILTS IS DOWN, WE MUST SAVE ON BOTH FOOD AND HEATING!
WHY CAN'T YOU SAVE FABRIC INSTEAD? SELL SHORTER KILTS!
WE TRIED, BUT OUR CUSTOMERS GOT EMBARRASSED!
AHEM!

THERE'LL BE NO SAVING ON FOOD AND HEATING AROUND HERE, MY GOOD MAN!

WHO ARE YOU, PRAY TELL?
I'M LADY MEDDLESON FROM THE CHELTENHAM CHARITABLE CHARITY FOR CHILDREN IN ENGLAND!
I SUSPECT THAT REPEATING THE ORGANIZATION'S NAME WOULD STRAIN YOUR OVERBURDENED MENTAL FACULTIES...

...BECAUSE NO SANE MAN WOULD DREAM OF MAKING CONDITIONS EVEN WORSE FOR THESE POOR CHILDREN!
I SAY PHOOEY TO SAVING, SIR! PHOOEY!

THIS IS MY BROTHER PERCY, BY THE WAY!
SAYING "PHOOEY" DOESN'T COST, BUT PEAT AND FOOD DO!

THAT IS WHY I TOOK THE LIBERTY OF BRINGING NOT JUST MY BROTHER, BUT ALSO THIS ENVELOPE!

THE 100 POUNDS IT CONTAINS WILL HELP YOU IMPROVE THE CONDITIONS OF THESE POOR YOUTHS!
ONE HUNDRED P-P-P...
NO, SIR, NOT ONE HUNDRED P-P-P! ONE HUNDRED POUNDS!

IF THE RESULTS PLEASE ME, I'LL DONATE EVEN MORE!
EVEN MORE? IS THERE ANY MORE MONEY LEFT IN THE WORLD?!

ACTUALLY I THINK IT WOULD BE NICE FOR THE GIRLS TO CELEBRATE A TRADITIONAL ENGLISH CHRISTMAS, NOT JUST THE HOGMANAY!
THE HOGMANAY?
YES, SIR, THE HOGMANAY!

CELEBRATIONS OF CHRISTMAS ARE BANNED* HERE IN SCOTLAND! WE CELEBRATE HOGMANAY INSTEAD!
?
* CHRISTMAS DAY ONLY BECAME A PUBLIC HOLIDAY IN SCOTLAND IN 1958!

I SAY PHOOEY TO BANNING AND HUZZAH TO WHATEVER NEEDS TO BE CELEBRATED!
GET ON WITH THE IMPROVEMENTS, MR. JOLLY! NO SHILLY-SHALLYING!
HUZZAH!!!

IF YOU PROVE YOURSELF WORTHY OF ANOTHER DONATION, I'LL SEE TO IT THAT NOBODY CAN DENY THESE GIRLS EITHER CHRISTMAS OR HOGMANAY!
HUZZAH FOR POOR AND RAGGED LITTLE GIRLS!

RECEIVING SUCH A DONATION SEEMS LIKE A MIRACLE, MISS CRAMM! BUT WHAT WILL HAPPEN WHEN OUR LANDLORD MR. MACMISER FINDS OUT?
?

SPEAKING OF MIRACLES...SINCE WHEN DID DELIVERYMEN SUDDENLY START GROWING YOUNGER?!
EH...

NICE TO MEET YE, LAD! NOW GIT, OR I'LL CALL THE CONSTABULARY!

SORRY ABOUT THE SPLASH, POPPY LASS!
BUT IF YOU KNEW HOW THEY TREAT THE GIRLS INSIDE THAT ORPHANAGE, IT WOULD MAKE YOUR CHEEKS EVEN WETTER!

THE MONEY FROM THAT NICE ENGLISH LADY MAY IMPROVE THINGS, BUT MR. JOLLY SEEMS TO BE A PUSHOVER FOR HIS GREEDY LANDLORD!
ARE YOU ALL RIGHT?

I TRICKED MISS CRAMM INTO SENDING ME OUT ON AN ERRAND, BY SAYING WE NEED SEWING NEEDLES!
HOP ABOARD AND I'LL GIVE YOU A LIFT!

DIDN'T YOU SAY THAT THE MARKET FOR KILTS WAS DOWN?
YOU'RE RIGHT! AND THOSE ARE OUR KILTS!

IT SEEMS THAT ALL OVER TOWN, MEN PUT THEIR SCRAWNY KNEES ON DISPLAY BELOW A GARMENT OF OUR DESIGN!
SEWING EQUIPMENT & LADIES' WEAR

I'D LIKE A PACKET OF SEWING NEEDLES!
AND I'LL HAVE THAT BONNET AND FROCK, PLEASE!

WHAT ARE YOU DOING, SCROOGE?
I'M GOING TO INFILTRATE THE ORPHANAGE IN A MORE FITTING DISGUISE!

HOW DO I LOOK?
I GUESS IT'S CONVINCING!
WILL YOU GO TO THE HOGMANAY BALL WITH US?
WILL YOU? WILL YOU? WILL YOU?

DON'T BLOW YOUR COVER! WE POOR KIDS WOULD LOVE TO GO TO THAT BALL!
NOT WITH PESTS LIKE THEM!

WHAT DO YOU HOPE TO ACHIEVE BY GETTING BACK INSIDE?
I'LL TRY TO FIND OUT WHERE THE MONEY FOR THE KILTS DISAPPEARS TO!
AND ALSO TRY TO FIGURE OUT A WAY MR. JOLLY CAN STAND UP TO THAT AWFUL MR. MACMISER!

MISS CRAMM TRUSTED ME WITH THE KEY!

I DIDN'T KNOW YOU WEE LASSES WERE AT LIBERTY TO COME AND GO AS YOU PLEASE!
!!
OH, HELLO, MR. MACMISER, SIR!

I CAN'T SEEM TO RECALL SEEING *YOU* AROUND HERE BEFORE, MISSY?
EH...

UMM... I...MY NAME IS...UH...
THIS IS *PRUDENCE!* SHE'S A *NEW* GIRL!

I SEE...
EXCUSE US, MR. MACMISER! WE'D BETTER GET BACK TO–

QUITE RIGHT! YOU GIRLS SHOULD BE *WORKING!* ON YOUR WAY NOW!
YES, MR. MACMISER!

AH, *MR. MACMISER!* TAKE A LOAD OFF! MAY I OFFER YE A *CUPPA?*
SLAM

SPARE ME THE *PLEASANTRIES,* JOLLY! JUST PAY ME THE *RENT* YE OWE ME!
I'VE GOTTA HEAR THIS!

IF YOU GIVE ME *JUST A WEEK,* MR. MACMISER, I'LL HAVE THE MONEY FOR YE!
A WEEK?! DO I LOOK LIKE I'M MADE OUT OF TIME?!
PSST! MISS CRAMM'S COMING!

LOOK, MR. MACMISER! A CHARITY GAVE THE ORPHANAGE 100 POUNDS! IF WE SPEND IT RIGHT, THERE'S EVEN MORE TO COME!
I'M JUST BACK FROM THE SHOP, MISS CRAMM! HERE ARE THE NEEDLES AND YOUR KEY!
WHO'S THAT?

THREE DAYS, JOLLY! OR I'LL HAVE TO EVICT YOU AND THE GIRLS!
I'M PRUDENCE, MADAM! I'M A NEW GIRL!
ANOTHER MOUTH TO FEED! GO SHOW HER YOUR DUTIES!

OH, THANK YOU, MR. MACMISER! THANK YOU EVER SO MUCH!
COME WITH ME, PRUDY!

YOU'LL SOON GET THE HANG OF IT, PRUDY!
OUCH!
NOT SO LOUD! MISS CRAMM HAS EARS LIKE A HIGHLAND COW!

AH, MISS CRAMM! COULD YOU PLEASE GATHER THE GIRLS?
CERTAINLY, MR. JOLLY!

LISTEN UP, CHILDREN! MR. JOLLY HAS SOMETHING TO TELL YOU!
CLAP CLAP
HUZZAH!

THE ORPHANAGE IS BEHIND ON ITS RENT! IN TWO DAYS, LADY MEDDLESON RETURNS TO SEE IF IMPROVEMENTS HAVE BEEN MADE! IF WE CAN CONVINCE HER THEY HAVE, SHE'LL DONATE MORE MONEY! IF NOT...

...IF NOT...WE HAVE TO SHUT DOWN FOR GOOD!
?!
!!!

THE DAY OF THE VISIT! SCROOGE IS BACK IN DISGUISE...
NOW MAKE SURE YOU DON'T GET EVEN THE SMALLEST SMUDGE ON YOUR DRESSES! I'M RETURNING THEM TO THE SHOP AS SOON AS LADY MEDDLESON LEAVES!

I CAN'T WAIT TO SEE THE OTHER LASSES IN THEIR BONNIE DRESSES!
WHEN WILL THEY GET THEM, MR. JOLLY?
THEY WON'T, PRUDY! YOU THREE ARE THE ONLY GIRLS WHO LOOK NICE ENOUGH TO REPRESENT US!
!!

BUT THE OTHER GIRLS ARE IN THE PARLOR NOW!
THEY'RE JUST THERE TO HEAT UP THE ROOM BEFORE THE GUESTS ARRIVE!
JUMPING JACKS! ONE-TWO, ONE-TWO—
PUFF! PUFF! PUFF!

I'D GO FOR PEAT!
THERE'S NO MONEY FOR PEAT, PRUDENCE! NOW LOOK POSITIVE, LASSIES, AND WE MIGHT GET THE MONEY TO STAY ON!

DING-DONG
THAT WILL BE THEM NOW!
I'LL HIDE THE OTHER GIRLS, MR. JOLLY!

YOU STAY THERE! AND REMEMBER...NOT A WORD ABOUT WORK!

MY LADY! YOU HONOR THIS HOUSE!
PISH-TOSH! I'M JUST DOING MY DUTY TO HELP THOSE LESS FORTUNATE!
OH, IT MUST BE AWFUL NOT TO BE US!

PLEASE COME IN AND MEET SOME REPRE-SENTATIVE GIRLS!
HOW ARE YOU...
...LADY...
...MEDDLESON?
WELL, THEY LOOK ROSY-CHEEKED ENOUGH!
AND IT'S NICE AND WARM HERE, TOO!

DO YOU WANT A PIECE OF CAKE, MY LASS?
DON'T MIND IF I DO, MISS CRAMM!

YOUR HANDS FEEL ROUGH! YOU HAVEN'T BEEN WORKING, HAVE YOU?

CHILDREN ARE SUPPOSED TO BE IN SCHOOL, NOT DOING TOUGH CHORES!
UH...I GET CALLUSES FROM PLAYING THE PIANO!

IT LOOKS LIKE THINGS ARE IMPROVING AROUND HERE! BUT YOU COULD CERTAINLY USE A PIANO TUNER!
SOUNDS FINE TO ME!

OH, ABOUT CHRISTMAS...WE THOUGHT A ROAST TURKEY MIGHT BE THE TICKET!
SO IF YOU THINK YOU MIGHT FIND IT IN YOUR HEART TO LET THE POOR GIRLS CELEBRATE CHRISTMAS LIKE YOU DO IN THE SOUTH...

I THINK YOU'LL FIND 10,000 POUNDS ADEQUATE FOR BOTH CHRISTMAS AND HOGMANAY—AND MORE!
THE WHOLE HOGMANAY!

HOW CAN I EVER THANK YOU ENOUGH FOR THIS GENEROUS GIFT?
BY GIVING THE GIRLS A BETTER LIFE!
COME ON, PERCY! IT'S TIME WE HEAD BACK TO OUR HOTEL!
OOH! JUST IN TIME FOR SUPPER!

CONTINUE TO IMPROVE, AND YOU MAY FIND YOURSELF THE RECIPIENT OF EVEN MORE MONEY FROM THE CHELTENHAM CHARITABLE CHARITY FOR CHILDREN!
IF I COULD GET MY TONGUE AROUND THAT NAME, I WOULD SING ITS PRAISES!

GIRLS, RETURN YOUR DRESSES TO MISS CRAMM AND YOURSELVES TO WORK!
SLAM

I'LL BURDEN MYSELF WITH YET ANOTHER TRIP TO MR. MACMISER IN ORDER TO PAY OUR DEBT!

YOU HAVE TO STAND UP TO THAT CROOKED LANDLORD, MR. JOLLY!
THE RENT IS RAISED AS OFTEN AS A SHIPYARD CRANE BY THE CLYDE!* THAT CAN'T BE LEGAL!
* THE RIVER THAT FLOWS THROUGH GLASGOW!

YOU HAVE TO SPEND THE MONEY AS INTENDED, ON CELEBRATING CHRISTMAS AND HOGMANAY!
AND ON PEAT!

ALL RIGHT! I'LL GO TO MR. MACMISER AND DEMAND AN END TO HIS CRUEL LANDLORD WAYS!
HUZZAH!

WE'LL ACCOMPANY YOU FOR PROTECTION!
YOU'LL DO NOTHING OF THE SORT! YOU'LL STAY HERE!

SIGH!
WELL, BACK TO WORK!
WAIT A MINUTE!
CLICK

I'VE GOT A UNIVERSAL KEY THAT FITS ALL OF THE PEAT CELLARS I MAKE DELIVERIES TO!

I BET IT FITS THIS LOCK TOO!
CLICK

BRAVO, SCROOGE!

LOOK! MR. JOLLY IS GETTING IN THAT CLOSED CARRIAGE!
WE'LL FOLLOW WITH MY HORSE AND CART!

BY THE WAY, I DIDN'T KNOW THAT YOU ORPHANAGE GIRLS LEARNED TO PLAY THE PIANO!
WE DON'T! IT WAS ME WHO WAS OUT OF TUNE, NOT THE PIANO!

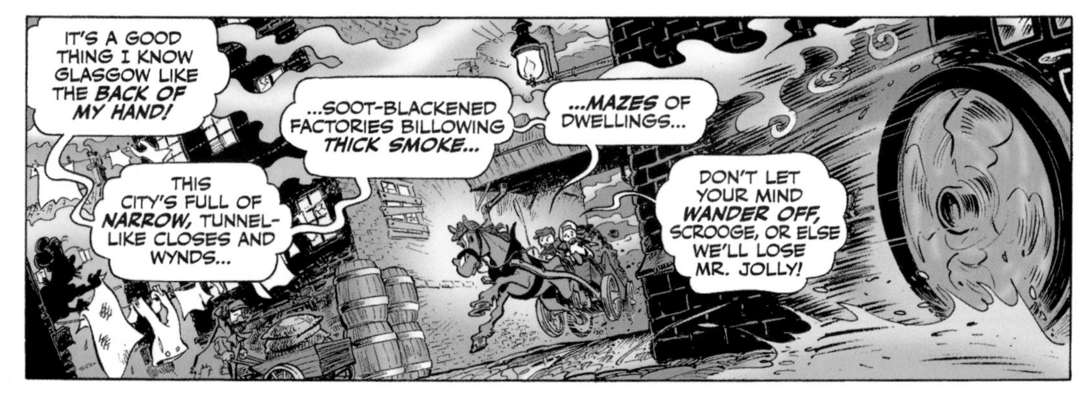
IT'S A GOOD THING I KNOW GLASGOW LIKE THE BACK OF MY HAND!
THIS CITY'S FULL OF NARROW, TUNNEL-LIKE CLOSES AND WYNDS...
...SOOT-BLACKENED FACTORIES BILLOWING THICK SMOKE...
...MAZES OF DWELLINGS...
DON'T LET YOUR MIND WANDER OFF, SCROOGE, OR ELSE WE'LL LOSE MR. JOLLY!

NOT TO WORRY! MR. JOLLY'S CARRIAGE JUST **STOPPED!**
SEEMS LIKE MR. MACMISER'S GOT A **SINISTER-LOOKING OFFICE** ON THE WATERFRONT BY THE CLYDE!

COME ON, LET'S SNEAK IN ON THE COATTAILS OF MR...

...MACMISER?!

THERE'S **NO ONE ELSE** IN THE CARRIAGE!
B-BUT **HOW?!**

MAYBE A **HENCHMAN** LED JOLLY OUT OF THE CARRIAGE IN A **DARK ALLEY** WHILE MACMISER **TOOK HIS PLACE?**
SLAM

IF MR. JOLLY'S **CAPTURED,** WE NEED **HELP!** I'LL ASK FOR **LADY MEDDLESON** IN THE POSH HOTELS!
AYE, SHE OUGHT TO **KNOW** ABOUT THIS!

I'LL **STAY HERE** AND KEEP AN **EYE** ON–
SMOOCH
DO BE **CAREFUL,** SCROOGE!

OF CARE I'LL BE COURSEFUL, BRENDA! EH...I MEAN...

SHORTLY!
MacMISER HASN'T LEFT HIS OFFICE, LADY MEDDLESON!
WE'LL GET TO THE BOTTOM OF THIS!

BRENDA HAS TOLD ME ALL ABOUT MR. MacMISER'S CRUEL WAYS!
AND THAT WE SUSPECT HIM OF CAPTURING MR. JOLLY!

NOBODY TAKES FOOD OUT OF ORPHANS' MOUTHS WITHOUT ANSWERING TO ME!

MR. MacMISER! A WORD IF YOU PLEASE, SIR!
BANG

YOUR ALL-TOO-FREQUENT RENT INCREASES FOR THE ORPHANAGE ARE IMMORAL, IF NOT DOWNRIGHT ILLEGAL!
NOT TO MENTION THAT YOU MADE MR. JOLLY VANISH INTO THIN AIR! WHERE IS HE, SIR?!
NOW, NOW! IF YOU CAN BE SO KIND AS TO GIVE ME A MINUTE, I'LL EXPLAIN EVERYTHING...

WAIT! DO YOU RECOGNIZE THE SEALS ON THOSE ENVELOPES, LADY MEDDLESON?
YOU'VE TAKEN EVERYTHING WE GAVE MR. JOLLY!

QUITE RIGHT, MADAM! AND NOW I'VE GOT TO FLY!
CRASH

I'D LOVE TO STAY AND CHAT, BUT I HAVE A TICKET ON A STEAM PACKET TO AMERICA!
?!!
THIS IS AN OUTRAGE!
MWAHAHAHAH!

AFTER HIM!
BUT HOW? WE'RE GULP! THREE FLOORS UP!

THAT ROPE WAS PART OF A WELL-PLANNED GETAWAY!

SO LONG, SIMPLETONS!

I'LL GET US DOWN FROM HERE JUST AS QUICKLY!
FWEEEEET

!!!
WHINNNY!

NOW JUMP! THE PEAT WILL BREAK OUR FALL!
BUT I'M AFRAID OF HEIGHTS!

WHEN TIME IS OF THE ESSENCE, FEAR IS NOT AN OPTION!
PLEASE TELL ME WHEN IT IS TIME TO BE SCARED!
WHEEE!
PEAT, DON'T FAIL ME NOW!

IF HE'S GOING TO THE HARBOR, HE'LL GET THERE BY TRAIN!
WE'LL HAVE TO CUT HIM OFF BEFORE HE REACHES THE STATION!

THERE HE IS!

WHOA, POPPY!
CONFOUND IT! IT'S A DEAD END!

HE'S *TRAPPED!* THERE'S *NO WAY OUT* OF THAT ALLEY!

THEN LET'S HAVE A LITTLE *CHAT* WITH MR. MacMISER!

HELP...
?!

THAT SOUNDS LIKE–
A *TALKING CRATE?!*
MR. JOLLY!

WELL, I NEVER!
OH, IT WAS *TERRIBLE!* THAT HORRID MAN *HID* ME AWAY!

AND HE'S GOT THE *ORPHANS' MONEY!* YOU MUST GO TO THE HARBOR AND *STOP HIM!*
BUT HOW DID HE *GET OUT OF* THIS DEAD END?

FOLLOW ME! I KNOW WHICH WAY HE WENT!
I SMELL A *RAT!*

IS IT *THIS* ONE?
OI! *MR. JOLLY!*
?

WHAT ARE YOU WAITING FOR? THERE'S NO TIME TO LOSE!
THERE'S A BEARD TO LOSE!

!!
YANK

WHOOPS!
?!
I SAY! WHAT WHIPMANSHIP!
STAND STILL...OR WE'LL SEE IF YOUR NOSE IS REAL, TOO!
!!

HE AND MR. JOLLY ARE THE SAME PERSON!
SO THAT'S WHY WE NEVER SAW THEM TOGETHER!

YOU FORCED THE GIRLS TO WORK LONG HOURS AND EVEN STOLE THE MONEY I DONATED TO IMPROVE THEIR LOT!
THEY'RE ORPHANS! AREN'T THEY SUPPOSED TO LEAD A HARD-KNOCK LIFE?

YOU ROGUE! GET THE LAW, BRENDA!
AYE, THE LAW! AND SOON A NICE, SAFE JAIL!

I SAY LEAVE LAWS AND JAIL OUT OF THIS! DON'T FOLLOW ME... AND I'LL LET THE LASS GO WHEN I FEEL SAFE!
!!
GASP!

I BID YOU FAREWELL!
CRASH

WELL, I'M GLAD THAT'S SETTLED, THEN! NOW WE JUST HAVE TO WAIT FOR THE GIRL TO RETURN!
IT'S NOT SETTLED, PERCY! THAT CROOK CAN'T BE TRUSTED! AND I'LL NOT REST TILL WE'RE SURE BRENDA'S FREED!
ALERT THE POLICE! I'LL STOP HIM!

THIS IS A STEEL MILL! IMAGINE IF THEY HEATED THESE FURNACES WITH PEAT INSTEAD OF COKE! I'D MAKE A FORTUNE!

LET HER GO, MacMISER! YOU'RE NOT GETTING AWAY WITH THIS!
STICKING UP FOR YOUR FRIEND, EH?

I TOLD YOU NOT TO FOLLOW ME, LAD!
CHUNK
LOOK OUT!
MWAHAHAHA!
SPLOOCH
FSSSSSSSSS
GAMMON AND SPINACH!
I WON'T MAKE IT BACK TO THE DOORWAY!

FSSSS
JUST ENOUGH TIME TO...

SMACK

...DO MY LITTLE *TRICK!*

!!
WHAT YOU DID JUST NOW *GALVANIZED* MY RESOLVE TO STOP YOU, MACMISER!

HAR! WHY DON'T YOU RESOLVE TO *GROW WINGS* AND *FLY?*
WE'LL SEE ABOUT *THAT!*
SCROOGE... I'M...
SNAG

...FALLING!

WHOA!
!!
GRAB

HOLD ON, BRENDA, AND I'LL LOWER YOU DOWN NICE AND EASY ON THAT HEAP OF COKE!
WHAT AN IMPRESSIVE DISPLAY OF USELESS SKILLS, LAD!

I SEE RIGHT THROUGH YOU! YOU HAVE A SOFT HEART!
AND WHILE YOU'RE PLAYING SUBSTITUTE SANTA, I CAN MAKE A RUN FOR IT!

MWAHAHAHA-
CLANG

POOF
SCREECH!!

HE FORGOT HIS HAT!
CRUNCH

SHORTLY!
YOU'RE UNDER ARREST FOR FRAUD! D'YOU HEAR ME, SIR?
H-HAGGIS?
WE'VE RECOVERED ALL THE MONEY, LADY MEDDLESON!
SPLENDID!

THIS GIFT WILL BE PUT TO GOOD USE WHEN I TAKE OVER THE ORPHANAGE!
HUZZAH!!!

AND SO THE ORPHANS HAVE BOTH THEIR HOGMANAY AND THEIR NEW-FANGLED CHRISTMAS AFTER ALL, IN THE NOW-WARM-AND-COZY STRATHBUNGO HOUSE!
SNIFF! YOU CHILDREN ARE SO ELEGANT WHEN YOU'RE DRESSED UP TO THE NINES!
NOT ONLY DO WE GET TURKEY, BUT IT'S STUFFED AS WELL!
AND SO AM I! BURP!
MERRY CHRISTMAS!
LADY MEDDLESON SURE BOUGHT A LOT OF PEAT FROM YOU, SCROOGE!
AYE! ONE FINE DAY, I'LL BE THE ONE WHO CAN AFFORD A TICKET ON A SHIP TO AMERICA!

...AND THAT'S HOW I MADE SOMEBODY ELSE HAPPY AT CHRISTMAS!

MR. MACMISER SAW RIGHT THROUGH YOU!
WE HAVE TO HAND IT TO HIM!
YOU DO HAVE A SOFT HEART, UNCA SCROOGE!

DON'T YOU AGREE, UNCA DONALD?
ALL THAT STUFF HAPPENED A LONG TIME AGO, BOYS...
...BUT I GUESS I'LL GIVE HIM THE BENEFIT OF THE DOUBT!

COME AND HAVE SOME MORE TURKEY, UNCLE SCROOGE!
AT CHRISTMAS, BOTH ORPHANS AND OLD MISERS DESERVE TO BE HAPPY!
End

Originally published in *Donald Duck* Sunday comic Strip (USA, 1963)

SHH! THIS IS CRITICAL!

HMM... TEMPERATURE 72°... HUMIDITY NORMAL...
ENERGY PLUS: VOLUME - MASS
E+P/M √3,200

OKAY, PUT AN X TO MARK THE SPOT!
ROCK-STRATA LAWS
ENERGY PLUS VOLUME-MASS
E+P/M √3,200

NOW STAND BACK!
VELOCITY 20
ENERGY PLUS VOLUME-MASS
E+P/M √3,200
TINK!

VELOCITY 20
ENERGY PLUS VOLUME-MASS
E+P/M √3,200
CRACK!

YOU SAY SOMETHING WENT WRONG?
YES! THERE WAS SUPPOSED TO BE A MAN RIDING IT!
End

Originally published in *O Pato Donald* #992 (Brazil, 1970)

BAH! MORE LIKE *YOU'LL LOSE,* SAILING THAT SILLY *LILY!* AND SINCE IT'S NOT WORTH BEANS, *I'LL* TAKE THE $1000 *HIT!*

Y'ALL FORGOT TO RAISE ANCHOR, CAPTAIN! ⋛SNICKER! SNICKER!⋚

⋛HM!⋚ DOGGONED IF YOU AREN'T RIGHT!
HOIST AWAY, MEN!
S. GIL li

HOORAY! AT LAST WE'RE ON OUR WAY!
AYE! AND IN SECONDS WE'LL LEAVE THE DUTCHMAN IN THE DUST!
YOU HEAR THAT, ANNIE? CAP'N SCROOGE IS WINNIN' OUR BET FOR ME!
YARR, HE AIN'T! HE'S LOSIN'! I'M WINNIN'!
S.S. GILDED LILY

THE DUTCHMAN'S PICKED UP THE PACE! NOT WHILE I'M ALIVE! FULL SPEED AHEAD!

HEY! OUR "FULL" IS MORE LIKE HALF-EMPTY! HOW COME?
⋛TSK!⋚ IT MUST BE THAT LEAK IN OUR FURNACE PIPE!

⋛ACK!⋚ WHY DIDN'T YOU REPAIR THAT BEFORE WE RACED?
ER... 'CAUSE REPAIRS COST MONEY...

...AND I WON'T HAVE ANY MONEY TILL I WIN CAPTAIN ANNIE'S $1000!

WE'VE GOTTA STEM THAT STEAM-LACK, LADS! SEE ANY OLD *RAGS* AROUND?
HERE'S ONE, UNCA SCROOGE!

≷BLECCH!≶ THIS'LL HOLD US TILL WE WIN THE RACE—AND THEN WE'LL BUY A NEW PIPE AFTERWARD!

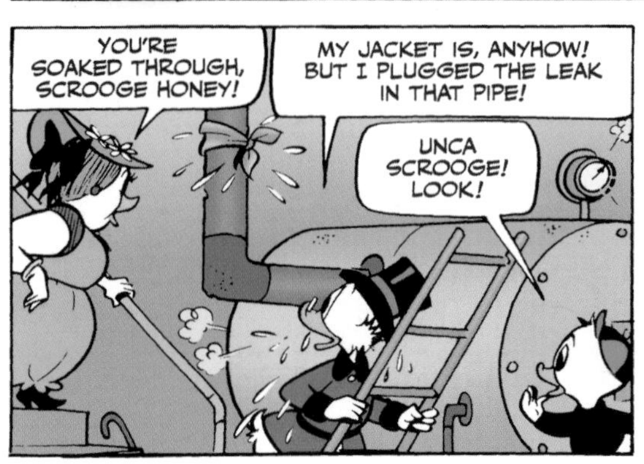
YOU'RE SOAKED THROUGH, SCROOGE HONEY!
MY JACKET IS, ANYHOW! BUT I PLUGGED THE LEAK IN THAT PIPE!
UNCA SCROOGE! LOOK!

≷GROAN!≶ WHAT IS IT *NOW?*
SEE! WE'RE NEAR OUT OF *WOOD* TO BURN FOR FUEL!

WELL, I DO DECLARE! FIREWOOD COSTS *MONEY*...AND I WON'T HAVE ANY *MONEY* TILL—

≷WAK!≶ BRING ME *WHATEVER WILL BURN,* LADS! I'LL REPLACE THE WHOLE WORKS ONCE WE'VE WON THE RACE!

CAN WE BURN THESE *CHAIRS,* MISS BELLE?
IF SCROOGIE'S REALLY BUYIN' *NEW* ONES...GO AHEAD!
I'LL LOOSEN THESE DECK PLANKS AND PRY THEM UP! YOU'VE GOT PLENTY TO SPARE!
EMERGENCY

HAVE WE PASSED THAT INFERNAL ANNIE YET, BELLE?
O' COURSE NOT, SCROOGE!

YOU'VE BEEN TOO BUSY WITH TH' FIRE TO MAN THE HELM! ≷HEH!≶ WHO KNOWS WHERE WE'VE BEEN SAILIN'?

WELL! WE GOT TURNED AROUND...AN' WE'RE JUST ABOUT BACK WHERE WE STARTED!
≷SCREECH!≶ MY $1000!
S.S. GILDED LILY

≷PUFF!≶ WELL, WE'RE HEADED THE RIGHT WAY NOW! EXCUSE THE SELF-INCRIMINATING QUESTION, BUT...WHERE'S THE DUTCHMAN?
UP YONDER! WAY UP YONDER!

TO BE PRECISE—IN TH' CANAL OFF PORTSIDE, PAST THAT ISLAND!
IF I DON'T THINK FAST, WE'LL BE STUCK BEHIND FOR GOOD!
HI, McDUCK...YOU OLD BABOON! IF YOU'RE GONNA GIVE UP THAT EASY, YOUR $1000 IS MINE!
CANAL
This Way

≷HMM!≶ MAP SAYS THAT CANAL ISN'T THE SHORTEST ROUTE TO GOOSETOWN! THE SHIPPING LANE BEHIND THE ISLAND—
IS A SHIPPING LANE, HONEY! IT'S RESTRICTED TO COMMERCIAL TRANSPORT!

≷GROWF!≶ I'VE GOT $1000 AT STAKE! I'M AS COMMERCIAL AS THEY COME!

DON'T MERGE TOO FAST INTO WATER TRAFFIC, SCROOGIE! YOU MIGHT NOT GET FINED...BUT YOU MIGHT GET RAMMED!

I CAN'T LOOK!
AT EASE, SAILOR GIRL! I KNOW WHAT I'M–
WAK!

HAWNK
THAT IS NOT A SIGHT I LIKE TO SEE OVERHEAD!

HAAWWWNNNNK
DON'T HIT ME! I OWN YOUR PARENT COMPANY!

I KNOW, McDUCK–I TOOK A PAY CUT WHEN YOU BOUGHT IT! I'M REPORTING YOU TO THE COAST GUARD!
THERE'S A $100 FINE FOR RECKLESS SAILING!
DON'T PANIC, SCROOGE...
I'M NOT PANICKED! IT COULDA BEEN $200!

HEH! YOU SURE LOOKED PANICKED IN THE SHADOW OF THAT SHIP!
HMPH! KEEP YOUR THEORIES TO YOURSELF!

SUBTRACTING $100 FROM $1000 MEANS I'LL HAVE $900 AFTER WE WIN THE RACE! THINK POSITIVELY!

IT'S A STRAIGHT SHOT TO GOOSETOWN FROM HERE! WHERE'S THE *DUTCHMAN?*
NOT TOO FAR AHEAD NOW!

SWELL! PRETTY SOON IT'LL BE ***WAY FAR BEHIND*** US!

LAND SAKES, SCROOGE! Y'ALL ***SHOULDN'T–***
DON'T ***DISTRACT*** ME! ANNIE AWAITS! ***FULL SPEED AHEAD!***

AWP!! WHY DO WE ALWAYS ***STOP*** WHEN I SAY THAT?
I ***TRIED*** TO EXPLAIN, BUT YOU SAID DON'T DISTRACT YOU!

SEE...WE SHOULDN'T HAVE GOTTEN ***CLOSE*** TO ANNIE AT TH' MOMENT! SHE'S ***STUCK*** IN–
A ***MUDBANK!*** AND NOW WE'RE ***STUCK TOO!***
S.S. GILDED LILY
YARR! ENJOYIN' THE VIEW?

JUS' FINE! HOW'S IT GOIN' WITH Y'ALL?
FAIR TO MIDDLIN'! I'LL ADMIT...I'M LOW ON ***FIREWOOD!***

NO BIGGIE, GIRL! BURN SOME O' ***MY*** CHAIRS AN' FLOORBOARDS! SCROOGIE'S REPLACING THEM AFTER THE RACE!

JUMPIN' JACKSNIPES! YOU'RE OFFERING HER **OUR** FIREWOOD?
SURE 'NOUGH! ANNIE CAN'T RUN TH' RACE WITHOUT **FUEL,** CAN SHE?

YARR! **BELLE!** WE'RE **STUCK** TILL **HIGH TIDE,** EITHER WAY— SO LET'S FORGET GOOSETOWN AND RACE BACK TO DUCKBURG **NOW!** SOUND GOOD?

MIGHTY SENSIBLE—
UNCA SCROOGE! THE *LILY'S* **LEAKIN'!**
GREAT HONK! WE'LL **SINK!**

FORGET MUD **AND** DUCKBURG AND GOOSETOWN! WE'RE TAKING ON WATER! **MAN THE PUMPS!**
DON'T **HAVE** PUMPS! PUMPS COST **MONEY**...AND I WON'T HAVE ANY **MONEY** TILL—

EEARGH! FINE! **WHATEVER!** YOU TAKE THE WHEEL, WHILE I **BAIL** WITH AN OLD-FASHIONED **BUCKET!** BETTER THAN THAT DAVY JONES' LOCKER!

WE'VE ONLY GOTTA STAY AFLOAT TILL **HIGH TIDE** AND **FREEDOM!**
WE'LL KEEP THE FURNACE GOING WHILE YOU WORK, UNCA SCROOGE!

MY WORK AIN'T WORKIN'! THIS BUCKET HAS A LEAK TOO!
HIGH TIDE'S HERE, GANG! WE'RE **OUTTA TH' MUD!**
START US MOVING, MISS BELLE! WE'VE GOT PLENTY OF FUEL NOW!

WHAT'S HAPPENING? HAVE WE OVERTAKEN THE FLYING DUTCHMAN?

WE'RE NECK AN' NECK! BUT YOU BETTER BAIL QUICKER–'CAUSE WE'RE SINKIN' FASTER!

HOW DO I GET MYSELF INTO THESE SCRAPES?

NEVER MIND–I REMEMBER! I'VE GOT $1000 TO HOLD ONTO!

GOSH ALL PETUNIAS...HERE THEY COME! THE FLYING DUTCHMAN'S LEADING THE RACE–NO, IT'S THE GILDED LILY!
FINISH
MAN THAT FURNACE, KIDS! KEEP BAILIN', SCROOGE!
FLY, DUTCHMAN... FLY!

TARNATION, WE DID IT! WE WON! TH' GILDED LILY IS FIRSTEST WITH THE MOSTEST!

THANK GOODNESS! WHEW! I COULDN'T HAVE BAILED ANOTHER DROP!

CONGRATULATIONS, BELLE! YOU WON ANNIE'S $1000—AND SAVED MY $1000 FOR ME!
FOR YOU? WELL...ER, YOU DID PROMISE ME A FEW THINGS!

LIKE BUYIN' A NEW FURNACE PIPE...AN' CHAIRS AN' FLOORBOARDS...AN' THERE'S ALSO THAT COAST GUARD FINE—

OH! AN' CAN I BORROW $1000 FOR ANNIE?
WHAT?!
YARR! YOU WON TH' BOAT RACE, BELLE!

BUT I DIDN'T HAVE TH' $1000 I BET YOU...AN' YOU DIDN'T HAVE TH' $1000 YOU BET ME!
'FRAID NOT, MATEY!

SO I GOTTA ASK YOU TO LOAN IT TO ANNIE, SUGAR—SO SHE CAN PAY ME TH' MONEY SHE LOST!

ƸGROAN!Ʒ HERE YOU GO... I THINK! BUT THIS IS TOO DEEP FOR ME, AND I'M SMARTER THAN THE SMARTIES!

AIN'T IT THE TRUTH? THANKS TO YOU, I'VE GOT $1000 TO IMPROVE THE GILDED LILY... AND IT'S STILL PART-YOURS AS COLLATERAL!
I'LL ADMIT... THAT SOUNDS GOOD! BUT I CAN'T RESIST THE FEELING I'VE BEEN TAKEN FOR A RIDE!
the End

Originally published in *Disney Anni D'Oro* #5 (Italy, 2009)

THERE! TRANSCRIBED THE ROUTE!
"HE HAD THE DOLL CONSTRUCTED AS A TALISMAN FOR THE EXPLORER BRAVE (OR GREEDY!) ENOUGH FOR THE TRIP!"

A FELLOW TRAILBLAZING ADVENTURER WOULDN'T SPIN TALL TALES!
$ $ $ $
JOURNAL of ADMIRAL BYRD
THE UNCHARTED ANTARCTIC
19

THANKS FOR THE CONSULTATION, CAP'N! QUITE AN INFORMATIVE READ!
YOU'RE ALWAYS WELCOME, MR. McDUCK!

HEH! GUESS I WAS THE FIRST IN YEARS TO SEE THAT PARTICULAR DIARY, EH?

ACTUALLY, YOU WERE THE SECOND IN FOUR DAYS! SOMEONE ELSE JUST REQUESTED IT! INTRIGUING, NO?
!?

INTRIGUING, YES! WHO REQUESTED THAT VOLUME JUST DAYS BEFORE ME? A STUDENT?
SOMEONE NAMED "POMP"... AND HE LOOKED A LITTLE OLD TO BE TAKING CLASSES!

GAH! BRIGITTA MUST'VE SHARED HER FIND WITH HER CORPORATE CRONY JUBAL POMP!
THAT WANNABE TYCOON KNOWS THOSE 24-KARAT BUZZARDS WILL GET HIM RICH QUICK...
U.S. NAVY RESEARCH CENTER

...AND I BET HE'D LOVE TO GO ON A FLIGHT OF FANCY TO CLAIM THEM!
NOT IF I CAN HELP IT!

I WASN'T PLANNING ON SUCH A HASTY DEPARTURE, BUT I HAVE NO CHOICE!
WAAHH... CHOO!

WHOOP! THAT'S SOME COLD YOU'VE GOT, NEPHEW!
...ACHOO!

SORRY, UNCLE SCROOGE! SNIFF! AS THE TEMPERATURE DROPS...
...SO DOES YOUR HEALTH! BUT SNIFFLES WON'T POSTPONE THIS TRIP!

TIME IS MONEY! I'M RACING TO A NEST OF ANCIENT GOLDEN BIRDS! WOULD MAKE ME A TIDY PROFIT... AND A BIT TO SPARE FOR YOU, TOO!
EEYAHH... CHOO!

THE ADVANTAGE IS OURS, BECAUSE I'M THE BETTER NAVIGATOR! WE'LL BE HEADED TO AN EXOTIC, SECLUDED LOCATION...
FANTASTIC! A CHANGE OF SCENERY WILL BE GOOD FOR MY COLD!

...RIGHT PAST THE SOUTH POLE! HOW'S THAT FOR A CHANGE OF SCENERY?
WAK!
WAHHCHOO!

WHAT'S THE MATTER? AFRAID OF A LITTLE CHILLY WEATHER? COME, DONALD, TIME'S A-WASTIN'!
ER, JUST A SECOND...

NEED TO LEAVE A NOTE FOR THE BOYS! SO THEY WON'T WORRY ABOUT ME!
DRAGGED OFF BY UNCLE SCROOGE ON CRAZY ANTARCTIC TREASURE HUNT. BACK SOON...? S.O.S.

COME, DONALD, THE TRIP WILL DO YOU GOOD!
IF WE WERE GOIN' TO THE SOUTH SEAS... BUT NOT THE SOUTH POLE!

ICE AND SNOW ARE THE LAST THINGS I NEED IN MY CONDITION!
BAH! THE POLAR AIR IS SMOG-FREE! IT'LL DO YOUR LUNGS SOME THERA-PEUTIC GOOD TO LEAVE DUCKBURG!

HEY! UNCA DONALD SENT US FOR COLD SUPPLIES SO HE WOULDN'T HAVE TO LEAVE HOME! BUT NOW—
AAAHHH...

SOMETHING STRANGE ABOUT THIS, MEN!
WONDER WHAT UNCA SCROOGE WANTS?
LET'S SEE IF WE CAN FIND ANY CLUES!

SOON!
GOTTA CHECK THAT THE BIN'S SECURE, THEN IT'S STRAIGHT FOR THE AIRPORT!
HAH-CHOO!

REGISTERED LETTER, MR. McDUCK! CAME YESTERDAY, BUT YOU WEREN'T HERE TO SIGN!
RAZZLE-FRAZZLE!
CLIK
CLAK

WHAT'S THE POINT OF THE POSTAL SERVICE IF WE POSTMEN DON'T FOLLOW PROTOCOL? IF THE WRONG HANDS GOT HOLD OF—
HAND IT OVER, SONNY!
Scrooge McDuck

WAK! IT'S FROM BRIGITTA! SHE'S ALREADY LEFT WITH JUBAL—TO FIND THE BIRDS AS A GIFT FOR ME!
WITH POMP GETTING A CUT!
EH... EH...

YOU COULDN'T HAVE LEFT THIS *YESTERDAY* WITH MY *SECRETARY!?* BEAT IT!
GEEZ, MAN.
AHH... CHOO!

PUT A SOCK IN THAT SNEEZING, DONALD! BRIGITTA AND POMP HAVE A *DAY'S HEAD START* ON US! AND I CAN'T *BEAR* TO SHARE *ANYTHING* WITH THAT WINDBAG!
-SNIF!-

SHORTLY!
-WHEEZE!-
PLANE IS READY FOR TAKEOFF, MR. McDUCK!
SWELL!
McDUCK INTERNATIONAL AIRPORT

OHO!
WHAT ARE *YOU*—
ANTARCTIC EXPLORERS...
...HUEY, LOUIE AND DEWEY...
...REPORTING, UNCA SCROOGE!

BAH! SCAMPER HOME, LADS!
NO WAY! WE'RE *VETERANS* OF HIGH-MOUNTAIN SURVIVAL COURSES—AND WE WON'T *LET* OUR UNCAS TRAVEL WITHOUT THEIR *JUNIOR WOODCHUCK GUIDES!*

WELL, SINCE YOUR UNCLE *DONALD* SURELY NEEDS A *GUIDE,* I APPOINT YOU—
AH... AH...

...OFFICIAL ASSISTANT HANDYMEN ON *OPERATION MIDAS FOWL!*
THANKS, UNCA SCROOGE!
CCHHOOO!

SCROOGE'S PLANE BEGINS ITS LONG JOURNEY TO THE VERY TIPPY-MOST-SOUTHERN-TOP OF THE SOUTH POLE...
...AND BROTHER, DO WE MEAN SOUTH! WHERE THE GLACIERS HAVE GLACIERS, AND EVEN THE PENGUINS SHIVER TILL THEY'RE BLUE!

AS THE DUCKS PASS THROUGH THE ORANGE AND PURPLE FLASHES OF THE AURORA AUSTRALIS, THEY APPROACH THE PHENOMENAL DESTINATION DESCRIBED IN ADMIRAL BYRD'S NOTES!
KA-CHOOF!

AT LAST...
LOOK! IT'S THE ICE VOLCANO!
RIGHT WHERE IT'S MARKED ON THE MAP!
THINK THERE'S REALLY A HOT SPRING AT THE COLDEST SPOT ON EARTH?
ONLY ONE WAY TO FIND OUT!
QUACKA-ROONIE! A NATURAL DEEP-FREEZE STEAM ROOM!
JUST LIKE ADMIRAL BYRD SAID!

AND THERE'S THE ISLAND HE MENTIONED!
THIS IS THE PLACE, ALL RIGHT!

A TROPICAL ISLE AT THE SOUTH POLE! AMAZING!
LOOK THERE! ON THE ISLAND...!
!

IT'S BRIGITTA AND JUBAL! HMMPH! LOOKS LIKE THEY THINK WE'RE THEIR SAVIORS!

THE FIRST BIRDS WE FIND ARE THE ROTTEN KIND FROM HOME!
HAND US THOSE BINOCULARS!

LOOK! FUNNY-LOOKIN' COCONUTS GROWING ON THAT PALM TREE! THEY WOULDN'T HAVE STARVED, UNCA SCROOGE!

AYE! AND IF THOSE TWO NINNIES CAN CLIMB A TREE, THEY CAN SURELY CLIMB A CRATER! THEY DON'T NEED US! RIGHT?

WHAT WERE THEIR QUALIFICATIONS TO VISIT AN UNCHARTED LAND? IT'S MY TERRITORY—

...OH, FINE! WE'LL RESCUE 'EM!
BUT HOW WILL WE?
WE CAN'T LAND IN THE CRATER!

NO PROBLEM! THIS AIRCRAFT COMES EQUIPPED WITH RETRACTABLE LANDING SKIS!
CLANNGK

AWK, AWRK, SKREEK! TRANSLATION: OH, BERTRAM! THOSE TWO TROUBLEMAKERS HAVE ATTRACTED EVEN MORE TROUBLE!
AWRK, SKRAWK, GERAK! TRANSLATION: GULP!

READY FOR LANDING, LADS?
R-READY!

SHHRUMMMPHH
WOW! MAKES THE MATTERHORN LOOK LIKE A MOLEHILL!

A PERFECT THREE-POINT LANDING!
BUT UNCA SCROOGE! HOW'LL WE ENTER THE VOLCANO FROM DOWN HERE?
SKRREEEEECH

FALL OUT! UNLIKE THOSE DUNDERHEADS, I CAME PREPARED...
CLICK

TO SCALE THAT SLOPE WITH YOUR BARE WEBBED FEET! THE FRUGAL WAY, RIGHT, UNK?
OF COURSE NOT!
CLANG

WE'LL TAKE THIS SPECIAL SNOWCAT I HAD GYRO RUSH-ORDER! LET'S GO!

PRETTY SLICK, EH? GYRO OUTDID HIMSELF THIS TIME! AND SO FAST!
...NO TIME TO PATENT IT...
WOW!
COWABUNGA!
YEE-HAH! AND AFTER THE CLIMB...
GULP! I HOPE GYRO REMEMBERED TO PUT BRAKES ON THIS SILLY THING!
...COMES THE FALL! BOMBS AWAY!!!
SKRAWK! TRANSLATION: WOE IS US!

NOW, AS FOR A MEANS OF CROSSING THIS BOILING WATER...
YEAH! NADA!

OH, NEPHEW OF LITTLE FAITH! THIS IS AN ALL-TERRAIN VEHICLE!
WAK!
SPLAASHH

WELL, WELL! SMALL WORLD, ISN'T IT?
SCROOGIE! MY KNIGHT IN SHINING ARMOR!
GRUNT! KEEP THAT TALK UP, AND I'LL LET YOU WALK HOME!
HOWDY, BRIGITTA!
YO!

OH, LAMMIEKINS, FORGIVE MY EXCITEMENT, BUT I'M SO GLAD YOU'RE—
SPARE IT! YOU OWE ME AN EXPLANATION!

CAREFUL! THIS WATER'S DARNED HOT!
WOW! NO KIDDIN'! A RIGHT SULFUR VAT!
CAREFUL, UNK!

COME ON, SCROOGIE! BEFORE WE TALK, LET'S HAVE A BITE TO EAT!
GROAN!
HEY, KIDS!

WHOA!
THIS ICE VOLCANO'S LIKE A SUPER DEHUMID-IFIER! MY PESKY COLD IS GONE!
A CHANGE IN CLIMATE WAS WHAT YOU NEEDED!

GATHER 'ROUND! THIS VEGETABLE SOUP IS JUST ABOUT DONE!
NOT SO MUCH VEGETABLE AS SEAWEED, BUT...

YOU'RE STRANDED WITH LITTLE FOOD, BUT HAPPY AS CLAMS! WHAT GIVES!?
NICE TO SEE THE POLAR AIR HAS CALMED UNCLE SCROOGE, TOO.

McDUCK, WE'RE HAPPY BECAUSE YOU'RE HERE! BUT THE PAST FEW DAYS HAVE BEEN NO PICNIC!
SO SCHLECK! WHAT'S YOUR STORY?
GOOD SOUP! NOM!
SLURP!

I'LL START, SCROOGIE! WE GOT HERE IN ONE PIECE... UNTIL OUR PLANE DECIDED TO CONK OUT!
SPUTTER!
SPUTT
I WAS SURE I PUT PLENTY OF FUEL IN THE TANK!

WE'RE GOIN' DOWN!
QUICK! THE PARACHUTES!

DANG! MY SUPPLIES!
SPLAASSHH

GAD! ONLY A JIGSAW PUZZLE GENIUS COULD FIX OUR RADIO TRANSMITTER!
FOOD'S WASHED AWAY! ALL THAT'S LEFT IS A PAN AND MATCHES!

"WE REALIZED OUR ONLY MEANS OF SURVIVAL WAS THE ONLY LIVING THING IN SIGHT: THE ISLAND'S PALM TREE!"

THESE LEAVES WILL BURN BETTER THAN DRY WOOD CAN!
AND ONCE WE BOIL THIS WATER, IT'LL MAKE AU NATURALE MINESTRONE SOUP!

ENTHRALLING STORY. BUT WHAT ABOUT THE WHOLE POINT OF THIS JOURNEY? THE BIRDS WITH THE GOLDEN FEATHERS?

BIG ZERO ON THAT SCORE!
WE FOLLOWED BYRD'S TRAIL AND FOUND NOTHING! HE MUSTA BEEN FUZZY IN THE WUZZY!
SCREEEEEECH!
AH, SWEET MUSIC!

SO THE EFFORT... THE INVESTMENT... MY RAGING BILE... IT WAS ALL FOR ZIP?!
MAYBE NOT! DEWEY CLIMBED UP THE TREE TO SEE IF HE COULD SPOT ANYTHING FROM ON HIGH...

AND LOOK WHAT I FOUND, GUYS!
A SIGN OF THOSE 24-KARAT PARROTS, MAYBE?

CLOSE! THESE COCONUTS! THEY MIGHT BE VERY OLD GOLDEN BIRD EGGS!
HOOT, MON! GIMME, GIMME, GIMME!

WITH A COATING LIKE REAL GOLD! BUT WE SHOULD HAVE AN EXPERT CHECK...
THE HONOR'S ALL MINE!
!
!

WOW! THE BIRDS' BIOLOGY ACTUALLY SYNTHESIZED A GOLD-LIKE MINERAL! SUCH A TRAGEDY THEY'RE EXTINCT...!

BUT AS WE WELL KNOW, SCROOGE IS WRONG!
SKRAWRK! TRANSLATION: NOT EXTINCT! ALIVE AND WELL!
KROWWWR! TRANSLATION: BUT HE DOESN'T KNOW IT!

JUBAL—ALL THE TIME WE WERE HERE, YOU NEVER NOTICED THOSE WERE EGGS?
WELL, FRANKLY, MY DEAR... NEITHER DID YOU!
...AM-I-RIGHT?

LET 'EM VENT, KIDS! ONCE THEY TUCKER OUT, WE CAN HEAD HOME!

UH-OH! WATER'S BUBBLING UP LIKE A POT OF BAKED BEANS!
BLUBBLE
BLUBB

YOW!
SO THIS IS AN ACTIVE VOLCANO, HUH?
LOOKS LIKE IT! WE GOTTA SCRAM!
BLUBBLE
BLUBBLE

I DIDN'T SIGN UP FOR THIS!
WE'LL FREEZE AND ROAST AT THE SAME TIME!
QUICK, SCROOGIE! LET'S GO!
WAK!

LOOK! THE PALM TREES ARE ALREADY WILTING FROM THE HEAT!
FORGET THE TREES... SAVE THE DUCKS!
BLUBBLE

AWRK! SKRAK! TRANSLATION: THEY'RE EGGNAPPERS BY MISTAKE!
SKRWAWK! TRANSLATION: GASP!

McDUCK, I HEREBY BEQUEATH YOU MY CLAIM TO THIS PLACE—IN EXCHANGE FOR SAVING ME FROM IT!
BUSINESS IS BUSINESS!
FULL SPEED AHEAD, LAMMIEKINS!

IT WASN'T A TOTAL LOSS! GOLD EGGS WILL PUT ME IN THE BLACK!
AND THEY PROVE BYRD'S STORY THAT THE BIRDS EXISTED!

DRIVE MORE CAREFULLY, McDUCK! I'M A-RIDIN' SIDE-SADDLE!

THESE ICE-WALLS COULD MELT AT ANY MOMENT!
DO YOU THINK IT WAS OUR FIRES THAT WOKE THE VOLCANO?
?

OOF! WELL—IF THEY DID, I'VE MORE THAN PAID MY PENANCE!

PHEW! SAY, IF WE SURVIVE, I THINK I'LL GO INTO RODEO!
AAH...

END OF THE LINE! C'MON, ALL ABOARD!
BRRRUMMBLE
CHOOOO!

SKREEK! RAWRRK! TRANSLATION: BERTRAM, WE MUST SAVE THEM!
GURRAWWK! TRANSLATION: BUT IF WE DO—THIS FROST WILL RUIN US ALL!

THE VOLCANO'S ABOUT TO BLOW!
DON'T WASTE TIME STATING THE OBVIOUS! GET GOIN'!
RUMBLE

HEY, DONALD, HOW'D YOU CATCH A COLD SO FAST?
BLESS YOU!
WAH-CHOO!

HEY! FLYING OUT OF THE CRATER! LOOKS LIKE EAGLES!
UNCA SCROOGE, THOSE AREN'T EAGLES—

IT'S THE GOLDEN BIRDS!
OH, MY STARS! LOOK AT THE SIZE OF 'EM!

SKREEK! SKRAWRK!
THE MICROCLIMATE OF THE VOLCANO MUST HAVE PREVENTED THEIR EXTINCTION!

OBOY! THEY WANT TO FURTHER PREVENT IT!
THEY'RE COMING TO JOIN US!

SWOOSH

VROOM...
WELL, McDUCK— LOOKS LIKE THE VENTURE WAS A SUCCESS!
AN EXPLORER EXTRAORDINAIRE LIKE BYRD COULD NEVER BE WRONG!
SLAM
WHIRRRRR

SORRY, PARENT-BIRDS! WE THOUGHT YOUR EGGS WERE ORPHANS!
BUT CAN THEY SAFELY HATCH THEM IN THIS COLD?
EHH...

EHHH-CHOOO!
CRRACK
CRACK

RAWK! SKREEK!
SKRAWRK!
WOW, DIG THAT SNEEZE POWER!
!!!
!!!

OH, HOW CUTE!
AND THE HATCHLINGS GIVE US A FULL SET! HEH!

THE SCIENTIFIC COMMUNITY WILL GIVE US A MINT FOR THIS PRE-HISTORIC FAMILY REUNION!
SO SWEET...
BUT, MR. POMP...
NOW'S NOT THE TIME TO THINK ABOUT PROFITS!
CHEEP CHEEP

PARDON THE INTERRUPTION, BUT THE OLD BIRDS' HOME IS ABOUT TO GO BLOOEY!
AH-AH-

AH-CHOO!
...CHOOOOO!

WELL! NOW WE KNOW WHAT CAUSED THE ERUPTION—THE VOLCANO CAUGHT A COLD!

THEY'RE SO TENDER AND DELICATE!
IN OUR COLD CALISOTA WEATHER...
...HOW WILL THE GOLDEN BIRDS SURVIVE OUTDOORS?
CRUNCH CRUNCH

I'VE GOT IT! BEFORE WE GO TO DUCKBURG, LET'S STOP IN FLORIDA!
THEY'LL BE A FANTASTIC ATTRACTION... LIVING IN TOTAL COMFORT!
WALT DISNEY WORLD
presents
The McDuck-MacBridge-Pomp Discovery
ARCHAEOPTERYX GOLDIUS

AND WE'LL LIVE IN COMFORT, TOO! EVEN THESE GOLDEN EGGSHELLS ARE WORTH A SMALL FORTUNE!
"WE"? HE SAID "WE!" THAT'S WHAT THE MAN SAID... THAT'S WHAT HE SAID... HE SAID THAT!
WELL—I'LL ONLY LIVE IN COMFORT WITH A FRESH BOX OF HANKIES! AHH...
AAHH-CHOOOO!
End

Walt Disney's Uncle $crooge in Going Medieval! Part 1 of 2

Originally published in *Anders And & Co.* #39-40/2003 (Denmark, 2003)

FOR COURTEOUS CONDUCT AND COPIOUS CONTRITION! THEY'RE MODEL INMATES, HE SAYS!
HEH! AND YOU DON'T BELIEVE THEY'VE REFORMED?

THEY'VE RE-FORMED INTO THEIR OLD CASH-THIEVING PACK! THAT'S AS PLAIN AS RAIN IN SPAIN!
BUT YOU'VE GOT YOUR SUPER-STRONG MONEY BIN TO KEEP YOU SAFE!

PAT! PAT!
BAH! CARE TO KNOW A SUPER-SECRET ABOUT THIS SUPER-STRONG BIN?
SUPER-YES?

KICK!
IT'S SUPER-FALLING-APART! CRACKS IN CONCRETE! FOUNDATION ROT!
CEILING INCOMING! CAN'T YOU FIX IT?

MY EXPERTS SAY IT'S TOO LATE! THE WHOLE THING COULD BE LEVELED WITH A TIN SLEDGEHAMMER!
SO YOU NEED A MONEY BIN MAKEOVER!

TELL ME SOMETHING I DON'T KNOW, NUMBSKULL!
THAT YOU NEED ANGER COUNSELING?

WEEKS GO BY!
SOUNDS LIKE A GREAT BIG CONVOY!
TRUCKIN' THROUGH DAYLIGHT?
TOOT! HONK! BLAAT!

YEAH—I'VE GOT A GREAT BIG CONVOY!
??!

IT AIN'T A BEAUTIFUL SIGHT! ENOUGH TRUCKS TO CLOG ALL OF DUCKBURG'S ARTERIES!
MY MOOLAH'S MOVING TO A SAFER PLACE. HOP ABOARD THE PACE-CAR OF THIS CARAVAN AND SEE!

WITH THE BIN CRUMBLING LIKE WEEK-OLD PASTRY, MY MONEY CAN'T STAY THERE!
BUT YOU'VE MOVED IT AROUND BEFORE. THAT TRICK NEVER WORKS!

YOUR CASH ALWAYS COMES BACK TO THE BIN IN THE END!
NOT THIS TIME! I'M SO CONFIDENT THAT I'LL MAKE YOU A DEAL!... BUT FIRST—

OBSERVE, DOUBTING DON! THE NEW HOME FOR THE McDUCK FORTUNE!
GOOD GOSH AND LITTLE GOLLIES! IT'S OLD FORT DUCKBURG! YOU'RE RENOVATING THAT MONSTROSITY?!

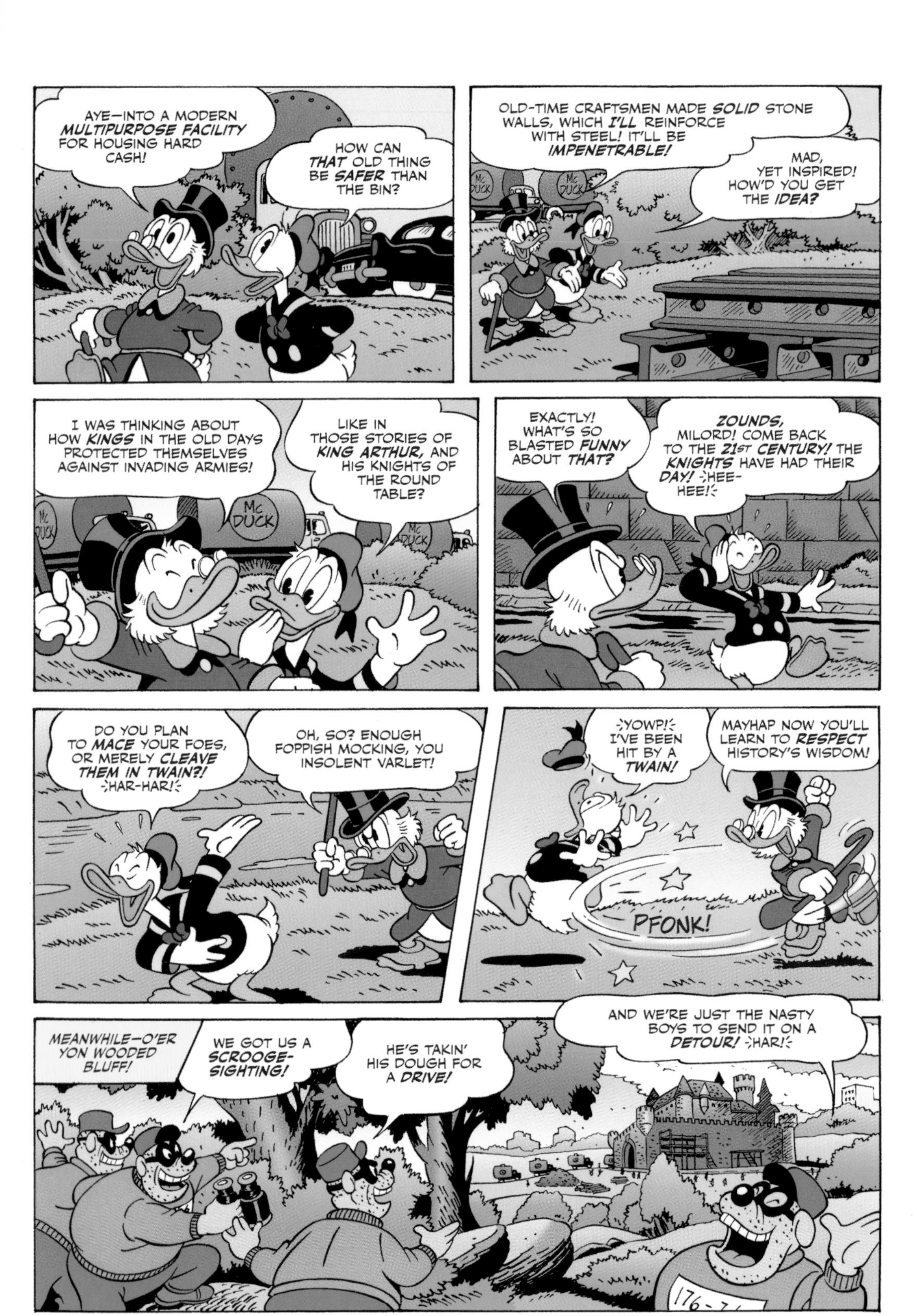
AYE—INTO A MODERN MULTIPURPOSE FACILITY FOR HOUSING HARD CASH!
HOW CAN THAT OLD THING BE SAFER THAN THE BIN?
OLD-TIME CRAFTSMEN MADE SOLID STONE WALLS, WHICH I'LL REINFORCE WITH STEEL! IT'LL BE IMPENETRABLE!
MAD, YET INSPIRED! HOW'D YOU GET THE IDEA?
I WAS THINKING ABOUT HOW KINGS IN THE OLD DAYS PROTECTED THEMSELVES AGAINST INVADING ARMIES!
LIKE IN THOSE STORIES OF KING ARTHUR, AND HIS KNIGHTS OF THE ROUND TABLE?
EXACTLY! WHAT'S SO BLASTED FUNNY ABOUT THAT?
ZOUNDS, MILORD! COME BACK TO THE 21ST CENTURY! THE KNIGHTS HAVE HAD THEIR DAY! HEE-HEE!
DO YOU PLAN TO MACE YOUR FOES, OR MERELY CLEAVE THEM IN TWAIN?! HAR-HAR!
OH, SO? ENOUGH FOPPISH MOCKING, YOU INSOLENT VARLET!
YOWP! I'VE BEEN HIT BY A TWAIN!
MAYHAP NOW YOU'LL LEARN TO RESPECT HISTORY'S WISDOM!
PFONK!
MEANWHILE—O'ER YON WOODED BLUFF!
WE GOT US A SCROOGE-SIGHTING!
HE'S TAKIN' HIS DOUGH FOR A DRIVE!
AND WE'RE JUST THE NASTY BOYS TO SEND IT ON A DETOUR! HAR!

WE'VE GOT MASTERS' DEGREES IN HIJACKING! BEFORE HE LOCKS HIS MONEY IN THAT CASTLE... LET'S SWOOP IN AN' STEAL IT ALL!
NOW? ARE YOU CRAZY? THE PLACE IS SWARMING WITH ARMED GUARDS!
176-7
76-671

THE WHOLE THING LOOKS LIKE SOMETHING OUT OF A MOVIE!
WHAT'S HE DOIN'? REMAKING "KNAVEHEART?"
176-

EUREKA! TAKE HEART YOURSELVES, KNAVES! WE'LL MAKE A MEDIEVAL MOVIE OF OUR OWN!
???

LISTEN UP, BROTHERS... ALL WE NEED TO DO IS BZZ! AND THEN BZZ! AND THEN BZZ!
ODS BODKINS, IT'S BRILLIANT!
HOLLYWOOD, HERE WE COMETH!

WEEKS COMETH, TOO... AND GO-ETH!
GRAB YOUR CAPS, BOYS! WE'VE GOT AN INVITATION!
TO WHAT?

HAR! THE LAIRD OF DUCKBURG, ALIAS UNCLE SCROOGE, IS HOLDING A CASTLE-WARMING!
HUH???

AND YOU SAY HE MADE YOU A DEAL?
I GET A $100 BONUS IF HIS MONEY'S BACK IN THE OLD BIN WITHIN NINETY DAYS!
313

YOUR FIRST BONUS SINCE EVER! HE MUST BE AWFULLY SURE!
FEH! HE'S MOVED THAT MOOLAH TO LAKES, FORESTS, AND EVEN OUTER SPACE—AND IT ALWAYS COMES HOME TO ROOST! THAT BONUS IS AS GOOD AS MINE!

STAND AGAPE, NEPHEWS, AT THE MIGHTY AND UNCONQUERABLE FORTRESS McDUCK!
WHOA! A REAL FORTRESS!
VERILY!

INVINCIBILITY AND PRACTICALITY IN ONE PERFECT PACKAGE!
THIS GATHERING CROWD SEEMS TO THINK SO! BUT I SAY PHOOEY!

WELL—BONUS IF YOU'RE RIGHT! BUT CROWDS DETER THIEVES... AND I'LL DOUSE YOU ON MY MEDIEVAL DUCKING STOOL IF YOU'RE WRONG!
HEE-HEE!

YOU PUT YOUR COMPLETE TRUST IN THIS MEDIEVAL TECHNOLOGY?
NOT ON YOUR BOILERPLATE, NEPHEW! OBSERVE YON TURRET! RADAR AND SURVEILLANCE CAMERAS!

I'VE FOUND THE PERFECT COMBINATION BETWEEN THE OLD AND THE NEW TO PROTECT MY MONEY!
YEAH? SO, WHERE ARE YOUR GUARDS?

OFF BEING FITTED FOR CHAINMAIL?
GUARDS ARE A NEEDLESS EXPENSE! NOBODY CAN ENTER EXCEPT ME!

THIS REMOTE RESPONDS ONLY TO MY FINGERPRINT! NOW, ALL ACROSS THE MOAT FOR THE GRAND TOUR!
CLICK!
CLACKETY-CLACKETY-CLACK!

NATURALLY, I'VE HAD THE PLACE FULLY WIRED FOR ELECTRICITY!
HMMM! I'M FEELING WORSE ABOUT OUR DEAL!
AND, AS THE CROWDS OUTSIDE STARE... I CLOSE THE DRAWBRIDGE, LEAVING US IN GREATER DUCKBURG'S MOST SECURE STRUCTURE!
CLICK!

WAK!

MEDIEVAL METHODS TO THE RESCUE!
LET THERE BE CANDLELIGHT!
WHAT HAPPENED?

JUST A BLACKOUT! NO ELECTRICITY, BUT WE'RE STILL SECURE!
I'LL CALL AN ELECTRICIAN!

NO SIGNAL! TELEPHONES ARE DOWN TOO!
THERE'S MY CUT-RATE, NON-SMART CELLPHONE...

GULP! EVEN ON CUT-RATE COVERAGE, I CAN TELL WE'RE BEING JAMMED!
WHAT COULD IT MEAN?
BZZZ-BZZZ!

CRASH!
EEP!
CHECK THAT! I KNOW...

TO THE TOWER, MEN! CALAMITY'S COME CALLING!
IT JUST TOOK NINETY SECONDS FOR DISASTER TO STRIKE!
GREAT HOWLING CRASHCHARIOTS!

THE TERRIBLE BEAGLE BOYS, AND THEY'VE GONE MEDIEVAL TOO! ...DARNED COPYCATS!
NOT NINETY DAYS. NOT NINETY HOURS, OR NINETY MINUTES!...
NINETY SECONDS... IT'S A NEW RECORD! BUT FOCUS, UNCA DONALD!

PHONE SCRAMBLERS, CABLE CUTTERS, CATAPULT AND BATTERING RAM!
THEY SURE DID MAKE THE MOST OF THOSE NINETY SECONDS!

BE SERIOUS! IT'S A FULL-FLEDGED INVASION!
ULP!
LET'S HOPE YOUR UNCONQUERABLE FORTRESS LIVES UP TO THE HYPE!

UNCLE $CROOGE in Going Medieval! Part 2 of 2

MOMENTS PASSETH!
WE SAW CHEAP, LOW-RES EMERGENCY FLARES FIRED!
WHAT'S GOIN' ON HERE?
WE'RE BEAGER BROS. LOW-BUDGET STUDIO, SHOOTING A FILM!

IT'S TH' AWESOME TALE OF A GREEDY BARON WHO GETS RAIDED FOR HIS ROYAL BOTTOM DOLLAR!
EFFECTS DON'T LOOK BOTTOM DOLLAR! NOT BAD!

I'LL LOOK FORWARD TO THIS PICTURE ONCE IT HITS THE THEATERS!
WHAT'S THE TITLE?
ER... "FALL OF THE HOUSE OF MISER!"

WHY, THOSE CLUELESS COPS ARE LEAVING! THEY REALLY THINK WE'RE FILMING A MOVIE!
SO WHAT NOW, O LEARNED LAIRD?

WITHOUT ELECTRICITY, ALL YOUR FANCY SAFEGUARDS ARE USELESS!
ELECTRICITY! SNORT! WE'LL DEFEND THE CASTLE LIKE KING ARTHUR DID IN DAYS OF YORE!

GET HELMETS! FIND WEAPONS! ANYTHING YOU CAN THINK OF, AND PREPARE FOR A BATTLE ROYAL!
YOU'RE BALMY! I'M NOT BATTLING ROYAL FOR YOUR DUSTY OLD MONEY!

YOU'LL BATTLE, OR HAVE A DINNER DATE WITH A DRAGON! GET GOIN'!
YEEK!
PFONK!

THE MOAT BRIDGE IS READY! BRING ON THE SIEGE LADDER!
LET THE INVASION BEGIN!
-YO-HO!- NO HASSLE BREACHING THIS CASTLE!

OH, SO? COAT THYSELVES WITH COOKING GREASE, SCOUNDRELS!
SLIMY WASTE FROM MY CAFETERIA'S FAKE-BACON NUGGETS!
GLORP!
-GLURG!-

-BLORP!-
SPLOOSH!
-YUCK!- I RECOGNIZE THAT FOUL TASTE FROM THE "McDUCK-BUCK MENU"!

NO FAIR, ENGAGING IN CALORIE-LADEN COUNTERMEASURES!
BUT WE HAVE OTHER GIMMICKS!

LIKE THE BEAGLE-FACED BATTERING-RAM!
ALIAS THE VISAGE OF VIOLENCE! CHARGE!

POUND!
POUND!
POUND!
POUND!
THAT BLACK-MASKED MAYHEM-MAKER IS WEAKENING THE WALLS!
OUR JUNIOR WOODCHUCK BOW SHOULD PUT A STOP TO THAT!

OUR FEARSOME FACE HAS CRACKED THE WALL!
NOW TH' COOP-DA-GRACIE! SAY GOODNIIIGHT—
AACK! FIRE FROM THE SKY!
ZIP!
TWANG!
RETREAT!

OUR WOODEN WEAPONS ARE WORTHLESS!
BUT WE'VE STILL GOT THE STONE CATAPULT!

WE'LL JUST PLAY "ROCK, PAPER, SCISSORS" WITH OL' SCROOGEY... AN' WE'LL BRING THE ROCKS!
FROM BEYOND ARROW-RANGE, TOO! NYAAAH!

ULP! THOSE AREN'T PAPIER-MÂCHÉ FILM-PROP BOULDERS, UNCA SCROOGE!
BUT OUR ROOF IS BUSTING LIKE PAPIER-MÂCHÉ!
BASH!

Y-YOUR ORDERS, SIRE?
JUST ONE! ABANDON SHIP... ER, FORTRESS!

YO-HO! THE DRAWBRIDGE LOWER-ETH IN DEFEAT!
VICTORY IS OURS!
CREEEAK!

YEE-HAARRR! TO THE TREASURE VAULTS—AND OUR ILL-GOTTEN GAINS, BRAVE BEAGLES!
AFTER WE TIE UP YON DUCK KNIGHTS!

MAKE WAY FOR OUR BIG BUCK TRUCK! YO-HO!
YO-HO! LET'S FILL IT UP WITH DOUGH!

OUR LI'L "MOVIE'S" GONNA SNAG AN ACADEMY AWARD! SAFECRACKERS' ACADEMY, THAT IS!
CROOKS! SCHLOCK PRODUCERS!

SOON ENOUGH!
THAT'S A WRAP! TH' TRUCK'S CRAMMED FULLA CASH!
NOW ON TO THE AFTERPARTY! HAR!

GOOD WORK, BOYS! THOSE BRIGANDS NEVER FOUND YOU AMONG THE DEBRIS!
UNTIE US, QUICK!

TOO LATE! THEY GOT AWAY, AND WE DON'T KNOW WHERE TO!
DRAT!

WHAT ARE YOU GAWKING AT? WHY DIDN'T YOU TRY TO STOP THE THIEVES?
THOSE BRAVE KNIGHTS?
BRAVE KNIGHTS WOULD NEVER BE THIEVES!

IDIOTS! THIS IS NO MOVIE! THIS IS REAL!
IS THIS TANTRUM PART OF THE MOVIE, TOO?
MUST BE A REHEARSAL! CAMERAMAN'S GONE HOME FOR THE DAY!

DISASTER! ALL IS LOST! SOB!
YOUR MONEY'S GONE, SO I WON'T GET MY BONUS! BUT I KNEW YOUR KING ARTHUR DREAM WAS A DUD!

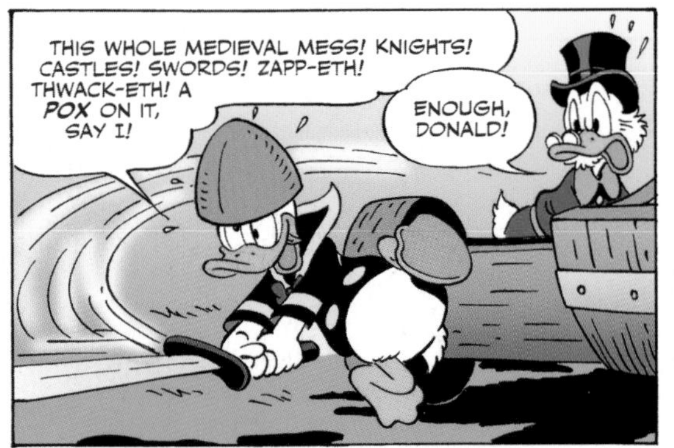
THIS WHOLE MEDIEVAL MESS! KNIGHTS! CASTLES! SWORDS! ZAPP-ETH! THWACK-ETH! A POX ON IT, SAY I!
ENOUGH, DONALD!

HISTORY'S WISDOM, HE SAYS! EGAD! WHAT DOES DONALD KNOW? HE'S JUST A FOOL WITH HIS HEAD IN THE...
I SAID ENOUGH!
SLAM!

...CLOUUUDDDS!
SPROINGG!

ER... OOPS-ETH?

MEANWHILE—OUR FIENDISH "FILMMAKERS" FURTIVELY FLEE!
VERILY, WE ROLL ALONG, ROLL ALONG, ROLL ALONG...
BEAGER BROS. PICTURES

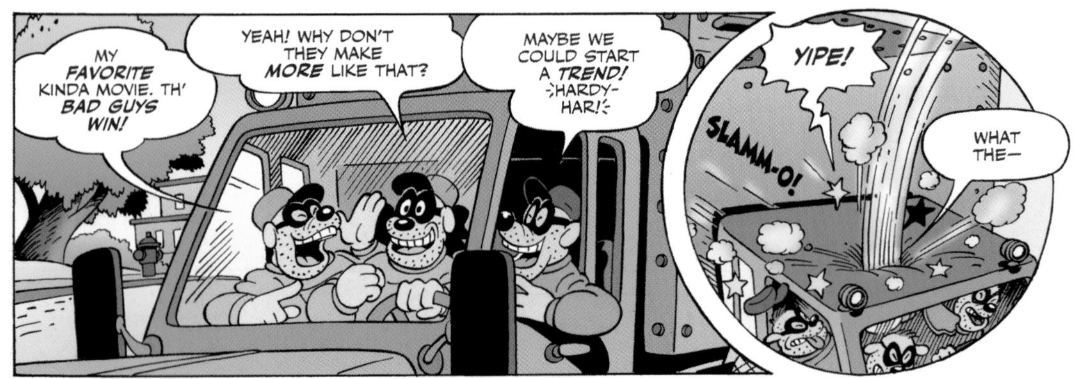
MY FAVORITE KINDA MOVIE. TH' BAD GUYS WIN!
YEAH! WHY DON'T THEY MAKE MORE LIKE THAT?
MAYBE WE COULD START A TREND! HARDY-HAR!
YIPE!
SLAMM-O!
WHAT THE—

UGH! WHO DECIDED TO CAST US IN "DUCK-NADO?"
I DUNNO... BUT GRAB TH' WHEEL! QUICK!

TSK! VIOLATION OF DUCKBURG'S TRAFFIC CODES!

OOOF!
URK!
BEAGER BROS. PICTURES
SMASH!
MY, MY! LITTERING... ILLEGAL PARKING... AND DON'T THOSE CADS KNOW THERE'S NO SLEEPING IN A PUBLIC PARK?

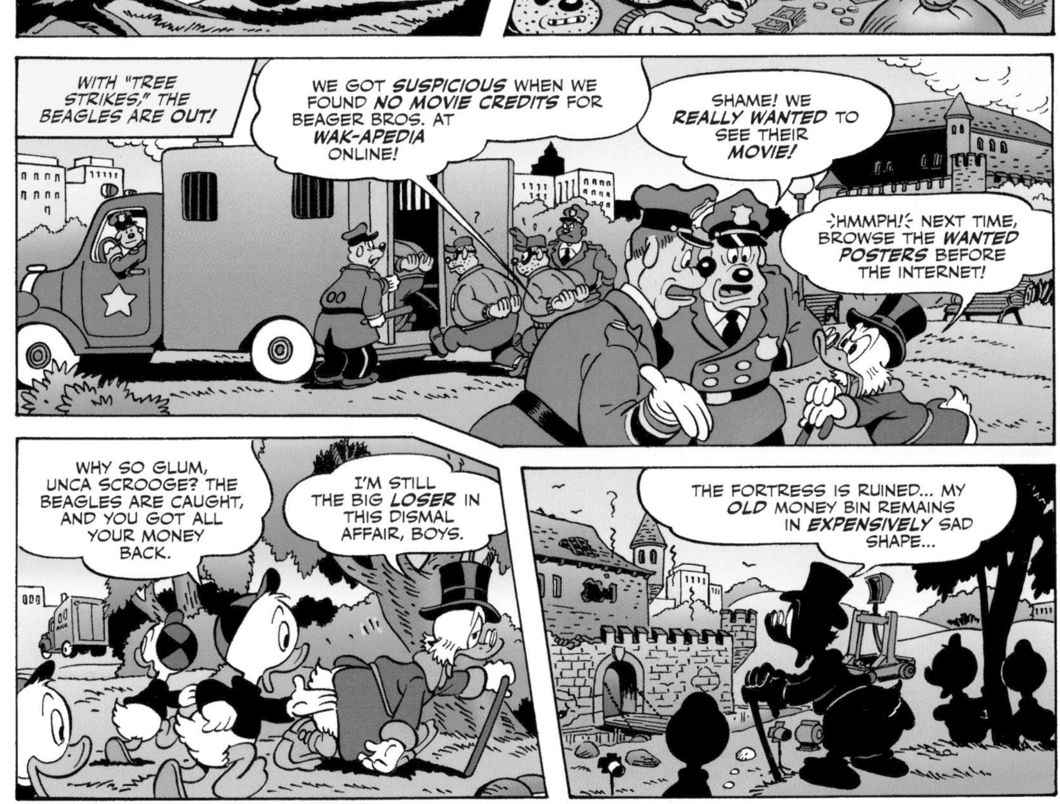
WITH "TREE STRIKES," THE BEAGLES ARE OUT!
WE GOT SUSPICIOUS WHEN WE FOUND NO MOVIE CREDITS FOR BEAGER BROS. AT WAK-APEDIA ONLINE!
SHAME! WE REALLY WANTED TO SEE THEIR MOVIE!
HMMPH! NEXT TIME, BROWSE THE WANTED POSTERS BEFORE THE INTERNET!
WHY SO GLUM, UNCA SCROOGE? THE BEAGLES ARE CAUGHT, AND YOU GOT ALL YOUR MONEY BACK.
I'M STILL THE BIG LOSER IN THIS DISMAL AFFAIR, BOYS.
THE FORTRESS IS RUINED... MY OLD MONEY BIN REMAINS IN EXPENSIVELY SAD SHAPE...

...AND THERE'S STILL THAT BONUS DEAL I HAVE WITH YOUR UNCLE DONALD! SIGH!
HEY! THIS MIGHT SOLVE IT ALL— BZZ! BZZ BZZ!
BRAVO!

JUST UNDER THREE MONTHS LATER!
SORRY YOUR DEAL FLOPPED, UNCA DONALD!
YEAH, I HAD A FEELING UNK WOULD FIND A WAY TO SKIRT THE 90-DAY "RETURN-TO-NORMAL" DEADLINE!

BUT THE BIN'S REPAIRED, HIS MONEY'S IN IT...
...AND LIFE GOES ON! HI, UNCA SCROOGE!
WELCOME, LADS, TO MY LATEST ATTRACTION!
313

QUACKA-ROONIES! YOU TURNED THE BACK BIN WALL INTO A DRIVE-IN THEATER...
...AND YOU'RE SHOWING THE BEAGLES' SHAM CASTLE-SIEGE MOVIE?!
YES... TO PUNISH THEM, THE POLICE AWARDED ME THE RIGHTS!
TONIGHT
SCROOGE McDUCK in "GAME OF SCONES!"
6961

PRESALES HAVE ALREADY COVERED MY BIN'S RECONSTRUCTION... BUT MY MONEY STAYED OUT FOR 91 DAYS! HEE-HEE!
UNCA DONALD, WHERE ARE YOU GOING?

HOME— BEFORE SOME TOP-HATTED TURNIP-SQUEEZER REMEMBERS MY APPOINTMENT WITH A DUCKING STOOL!

Ye End

Originally published in *Kalle Anka & C:o* #12/2012 (Sweden, 2012)

HAHA! YOU'RE UNDER MY SPELL! YOU HAVE TO OBEY MY COMMANDS, AND MY COMMANDS ONLY!

NOW, GO AND GET YOUR NUMBER ONE DIME AND GIVE IT TO ME!
OKAY...

AND DON'T SAY ANYTHING TO ANYONE WHILE GETTING IT!
AS YOU COMMAND...

DOGGONE! I'M REALLY UNDER THE SPELL! I CAN'T WARN THE GUARD NO MATTER HOW HARD I TRY!
WELCOME BACK, SIR! THAT WAS FAST!

BUT I'M STILL AWARE THAT I DON'T WANT TO GIVE THE DIME TO MAGICA!
WHICH MEANS I CAN STILL ACT AGAINST HER, EVEN THOUGH I HAVE TO OBEY HER COMMANDS!

HERE YOU GO, MAGICA... MY FIRST DIME AS ORDERED!
THANK YOU, SUCKER! HEE! HEE! HEE!
AND NOW— I'VE GOT YOUR WAND!
HEY!

NOW YOU HAVE TO OBEY MY COMMANDS, AND MY COMMANDS ONLY!
THIS IS UNFAIR! THAT'S MY WAND!
AND THAT'S MY DIME! I ORDER YOU TO GIVE IT BACK TO ME, AND TO REVERSE THE SPELL YOU CAST ON ME!
GRR!
I HAVE TO OBEY AND GIVE YOU BACK THE DIME, BUT THE SPELL CAN'T BE REVERSED UNLESS YOU BREAK THE WAND—AND IT'S INDESTRUCTIBLE!

FLING!
YOUR COMMAND FORCES ME TO TELL YOU THAT THE SPELL WILL WEAR OFF IN HALF AN HOUR AND— HEY! I PAID A LOT FOR THAT WAND!
GRR! YOU'RE STILL UNDER MY SPELL, SO I ORDER YOU TO GIVE ME BACK THE DIME!

OKAY, I HAVE TO OBEY THAT ORDER, BUT YOU'RE ALSO STILL UNDER MY SPELL, AND I ORDER YOU NOT TO TAKE IT... TO FLEE FROM THE DIME!

OKAY, BUT WHILE I OBEY YOUR ORDER, I ORDER YOU TO CATCH ME AND GIVE THE DIME TO ME BY ANY MEANS NECESSARY!
!

HURRY UP!
THIS IS RIDICULOUS! I HAVE TO COME UP WITH SOMETHING TO STOP MYSELF FROM REACHING MAGICA!
GOT IT!
MAGICA! I ORDER YOU TO FOOF-BOMB ME!

OKAY, BUT IN THAT CASE, I ORDER YOU TO DODGE!
DARN! I HAVE TO OBEY!
FOOF!
OH, WHAT A SHAME! I MISSED!

SO THE CHASE GOES ON UNTIL— HEY, A FIRE HYDRANT!
OWCH!
KICK!

YOU'RE CHEATING AGAIN, McDUCK!
WELL, YOU DIDN'T FORBID ME TO HURT MYSELF! "TOO BAD" I CAN'T RUN WITH THIS FOOT!

BUT PLEASE, DON'T STOP FOR ME... AND THAT'S AN ORDER!
NOW I HAVE TO HURT MYSELF TOO, TO NOT GET AWAY!
OWOOCH!
KICK!

NOW I'M ALSO HURT AND CAN'T RUN! BUT I ORDER YOU TO CHASE ME BY HOPPING ON ONE LEG FROM NOW ON!
!

IN THAT CASE, I ORDER YOU TO ESCAPE BY HOPPING AWAY!
GRR!

WE'RE NOT GETTING ANYWHERE! SCROOGE WILL NEVER CATCH ME LIKE— HEY, I'VE GOT AN IDEA!
HOP
HOP
HOP

SCROOGE, I COMMAND YOU TO COMMAND ME TO CRAWL, AND NOT TO COMMAND ME TO COMMAND YOU TO DO ANYTHING THAT WOULD SLOW YOU DOWN!
GULP!

GRR! SINCE I HAVE TO OBEY, I COMMAND YOU TO CRAWL!
I'LL GLADLY OBEY YOUR COMMAND!

AND I CAN'T COMMAND HER TO COMMAND ME TO CRAWL, TOO! EVEN HOPPING, I'LL CATCH HER IN A FEW SECONDS! DARN DARN DARN...

HM!
?

HAH! SEEING THAT LITTLE KID GAVE ME AN IDEA! MAGICA, I ORDER YOU TO BE A GOOD LITTLE KID FROM NOW ON, AND NOT A TERRIBLE SORCERESS!

HERE'S MY NUMBER ONE DIME! BECAUSE OF THE SPELL AND YOUR COMMAND, I HAVE TO GIVE IT TO YOU!

BY THE FIRES OF VESUVIUS! BECAUSE OF THE SPELL, I HAVE TO OBEY HIS ORDER TO BE A "GOOD LITTLE KID"!

HERE—I CAN'T TAKE YOUR DIME! I KNOW HOW MUCH IT MEANS TO YOU!
HEE-HEE! THAT'S MY GOOD LITTLE KID! THANK YOU VERY MUCH!

BING

PERFECT! I GOT RELEASED FROM THE SPELL AND GOT MY DIME BACK AT THE SAME TIME!

I HEXED MAGICA ABOUT TEN MINUTES AFTER SHE HEXED ME! THAT GIVES ME MORE THAN ENOUGH TIME TO GET MY DIME SAFELY BACK IN THE MONEY BIN BEFORE SHE COMES TO HERSELF AGAIN!

WAIT! MY DIME! WHERE IS IT? WHERE DID I PUT IT?

WAK! THERE'S A HOLE IN MY POCKET!
IS SOMETHING WRONG, BOSS?

I DROPPED MY NUMBER ONE DIME SOMEWHERE! HELP ME FIND IT!

A DIME, YOU SAY? I DON'T SEE ONE!
MR. McDUCK!
?

HERE'S YOUR DIME BACK! I SAW IT FALL FROM YOUR POCKET AND SINCE I'M A GOOD LITTLE KID, I PICKED IT UP TO RETURN IT TO YOU!

I KNOW HOW MUCH IT MEANS TO YOU!
THAT WAS THE "TERRIBLE SORCERESS" YOU'RE SO AFRAID OF?!! BWAHAHAHA!
End

Art by Fabrizio Petrossi, Colors by Ronda Pattison

Art by Ulrich Schroeder, Colors by Sanoma

Art by Andrea Freccero, Colors by Mario Perrotta

Art by Marco Gervasio, Colors by Marco Colletti

Art by Marco Rota, Colors by Marco Colletti

Art by Silvia Ziche, Colors by Egmont and David Gerstein

Art by Massimo Fecchi, Colors by Marco Colletti

Art by Andrea Freccero, Colors by Max Monteduro